Stazy and the Magic List

By
Nancy Hundal

Published by Rebel Mountain Press, 2023
Copyright © 2023 by Nancy Hundal

Cover Art & Design—Karen Holland
Edited by Lori Shwydky, Rebel Mountain Press

Library and Archives Canada Cataloguing in Publication

Title: Stazy and the magic list / Nancy Hundal.
Names: Hundal, Nancy, 1957- author.
Identifiers: Canadiana 20230166709 | ISBN 9781989996157 (softcover)
Classification: LCC PS8565.U5635 S59 2023 | DDC jC813/.54—dc23

Printed and bound in Canada

ISBN 978-1-989996-15-7 (softcover)
Rebel Mountain Press—Nanoose Bay, BC, Canada

*We gratefully acknowledge and appreciate that we are located on the traditional territory of the
Snaw-Naw-As First Nation.*

We gratefully acknowledge the support of

Supported by the Province of British Columbia

www.rebelmountainpress.com

To Karen and Kirk—a magical pair
and
to my McKechnie family,
with whom I had 34 years of kids and books
. . . and a little stardust thrown in from time to time.

"And above all, watch with glittering eyes the whole world around you because the greatest secrets are always hidden in the most unlikely places. Those who don't believe in magic will never find it."

~ Roald Dahl

Part 1

Back to School

Stazy

Why?

The door opened with a nasty *hisss*, and I felt every eye in the room slide from the tall figure at the front to me. Now the faceless adult was talking at me, but I felt frozen, my lips crumpled into a pre-vomit smile.

Why do they do this to kids? I came early, like they said; I waited in the office while phones rang, papers shuffled from one hand to another, and adults leaned down to encourage, coax, or bully kids who looked back at them in jittery mixes of horror and terror. I was the only kid alone.

But why the half hour early? More time for the butterflies in my stomach to play roller derby? I thought it was to get to the classroom early, so I wouldn't have to be the new kid on display at the front of the room five minutes after the bell rang.

Nope. There I was, pinned and scrutinized like one of my belly butterflies in a display case. Oh well; might as well get used to it. When my other . . . differences announced themselves, I'd have to get used to stares, yet again.

The tall adult—Ms. Burnside? Is that what she'd called herself? She pointed to a seat by the window. I skulked over. Best thing that had happened so far. Not only was I escaping the solar flare of Grade Seven eyeballs, I'd also lucked into a seat where I'd be able to stare out the window when things got rough.

Which, of course, was just a matter of time.

Rena

Doggone it! The new girl looked like more fun than a fresh pair of cowboy boots in a dung pile. Huge black glasses, black pigtails, funky black army boots, and a cool black cape thing; in fact, everything black except for these crazy orange stripes on her black tights. Checking out her outfit made me remember my own "first day" gear, and I couldn't help but sneak another little peek downward.

Wow—the leather fringe on my skirt exactly matched the one on my cowboy boots. How lucky was that! It was tragic that Ms. Burnside had made me take off my mini Stetson, but it was waiting there in my locker, ready to reunite the whole glorious outfit at break time.

I was rechecking my boots when that black pair came into view one desk over. Then the new girl's bag and bottom hit the floor and chair at the same moment, like a giant sigh. Of course, everybody was still staring. It was, after all, the first day of Grade Seven, and everyone was a little edgy. What could be better than gawking at someone even more nervous than you?

I flicked my eyes in Hali's direction. Her eyebrows were lifted sky high, as if she couldn't quite believe the new girl's outfit. And Faye? Between her perfectly-cut bob and the string of pearls around her neck, Faye's eyes bulged slightly as she looked over at me.

My quick survey convinced me that the new girl was *not* making the best first impression, so I turned to her and flashed my most angelic smile. Behind her thick glasses, the girl's huge eyes—were *they* black too?—hung onto mine for a second, but her mouth didn't change from that rubber smile.

Poor kid.

But then I started to feel that thickening in my throat, as a whiff of something breezed in with the girl. First one cough, then another, then another.

Not again! Asthma was ruining my life.

Air! Give me air!

Faye

Not only did she look strange, but she must have smelled terrible because as soon as she sat down beside Rena, Rena's coughing started. She was hacking so much that the crazy fringes on her skirt were whipping up and down like leather yo-yos. I was just jumping up to see if she needed water when Ms. Burnside said, "Hali, could you please take Serene down the hall to the nurse's office?" Rena would hate that; not even ten minutes into school and she was already watching the world go by from the sick-room door.

It shouldn't have surprised me though. Of course they would have told Ms. Burnside all about us, that we were the ones to watch for, the weird ones. They thought they knew all about us, but there was so much more to it. That no one could ever, ever find out.

I fingered my pearls and sat up a little straighter, forcing my brain to concentrate on what the teacher was saying. I ran my fingers over each pearl, counting them, banging them up and down against my neck. It was already boring, and I'd only survived thirty minutes of Grade Seven. Focus, Faye, focus! I locked my eyes on Ms. Burnside, heard something coming out of her mouth about homework. Oh no, not homework already. I tried tapping my fingers on the table, working out a little rhythm, then tapping my heels lightly for the big beats.

"Faye? What's all the noise about?"

Not so lightly, I guess.

I slouched back in my chair. *Yup, yup, yup.* Another long year.

Stazy

Homework? On the first day of school? Hopefully it wasn't reading. Or spelling. Or writing.

"Our first assignment will be a six-word memoir. Now, I can see all your eyes crossing at the thought of homework, but this is only six words!" If this was anything like my last school, everyone would be too polite or nervous to react to homework today, but by November there'd be a little cloud of moans, and by March a *groanblast* would follow any mention of the "h" word.

Ms. Burnside leaned back in her chair, really getting into her description. "There's a tale that the amazing author Ernest Hemingway was once asked to write a story in six words. He did, and here it is."

7

On the whiteboard were the words; six of them, I guess. Of course, I couldn't read them. As usual, the words were sliding and jumping around, making them impossible for me to understand. I squinted, I tilted my head sideways. Nothing.

I pretended to copy them onto the paper she'd given us, while she went on and on and on about how Hemingway had captured so much in just those words, how a whole world of possibilities was contained in them. Luckily, at one point she said the words out loud. They were, *For sale, Baby shoes, Never worn.* I said the words over and over, memorizing them, and as I did, I kind of got what Ms. Burnside meant. There *was* a lot in those words. But he was a famous author; easy for him! What was *I* going to write?

"So remember—six words about a significant part of your summer. Use those words wisely! We'll be doing this from time to time over the course of the year, and collecting them as a memento of your year in Grade Seven."

Great. Six words here, six words there. How about *New kid's perfume kills nearby cowgirl?* Nope, not about the summer. How about *New school, no friends, no chance?*

My six-wording was halted by a whizz of yellow and black buzzing past my nose. I watched it, curious. At least this wasn't the kind of classroom where an insect caused a shrieking stampede out the door. A couple of girls turned their heads, but no one else seemed to notice. Which was kind of weird, 'cuz it was a really loud buzz.

I did my best to blend in, even though that's hard to do in black-and-orange striped tights. (So why did I wear those tights, if they made the first day even harder? Because they were a little me-flag, a secret sign of who I was. I *needed* those tights.) A couple of times I got up enough nerve to look around for prospective friends, but let's just say that no one leapt out at me as an excellent possibility. The only person who'd bothered to smile at me had been led away to the nurse's office by an amazing-looking red-haired girl who I think had sniffed at me when she came to collect her coughing friend. I guessed

8

that people here didn't appreciate the spicy undertones of my signature scent, Bewitched. The girl with the green-striped hair and pearls—who wears pearls in seventh grade?—kept taking sneaky glances my way, but she didn't exactly look friendly, either. Everyone else was either listening raptly to the teacher, or looking stunned at being back in school.

Maybe one of the stunned ones would do for a friend.

Hali

Alas, the first day back didn't go quite as we'd planned. First that new girl, Anastasia, showed up and Ms. B put her by Rena, which destroyed the seating plan we were working on. "Alphabetical order," she said. "Disaster," we said.

We'd spent a lot of time online researching Faye's new look for school. She kept saying that this year would be different, that she wanted to concentrate better at school. So we found this conservative look to encourage her new studious, focused self. I was thrilled, because I'd love to have a study buddy. Her look was a bit of a mishmash, as she still had the greeny hair, but a greeny bob was better than her never-brushed look. She added the pearls herself, which was a little over the top. But that's Faye!

By lunch I was fairly sure she'd be back to sweats by the next morning, because the pearls didn't prevent Ms. Burnside from having to speak to her three times. On the first day!

It was an onerous day. That was my word for today, and it means troublesome.

The worst came last. In the final period Rena, Faye, and I had to go to a meeting for the Skills Class. Everyone watched us leave, like we were going off to be sprayed for cooties. And as if that wasn't enough, Ms. Burnside called out another name to join us—all year—in the class.

My hearing aids must have been turned up, because I heard it loud and clear: Anastasia. Stazy.

Stazy

I knew I'd end up in some special class, but I didn't think they'd scoop me out the first day. And if I'd had to pick fellow inmates, it sure wouldn't have been the coughing girl, her snobby red-haired friend, and the Pearl Girl. Nobody asked, though.

The group meeting was the usual *blah, blah, blah* about achieving potential, but I couldn't concentrate because of a bumblebee that made little buzzy circles over the Pearl Girl. Two bumblebees in one school in one day? I seemed to be the only one noticing, so I decided not to mention it.

Finally, the day was over. I stood at the school's double doors and asked my stripy orange legs for the way "home". It didn't feel like home, but that was something else nobody had asked me about. My legs knew, of course, and we headed off to where my toes had pointed.

The street was pretty nice; giant trees made an archway over my head, and I guess no one had told them it was fall yet because they were still a deep green. The lawns were like velvet, and behind them, houses looked cared-for and busy. I thought of my house, empty and quiet, with Mom at work. I felt again for the key hanging on a chain inside my shirt.

With my looking around at all this, I didn't see that those girls were ahead of me until I caught the cowgirl, walking in the middle, turning around to give me a quick smile. I think it was a quick, sneaky smile, 'cuz I don't think she wanted the other two to see.

To tell the truth, it was a little hard to see her face at all under that white cowboy hat.

Rena

I wish I'd said something, called out to Stazy instead of just looking back at her. I know she saw me, but she pretended not to.

It was just that Faye was bummed out over being hyper the first day, and Hali kept saying what an onerous day it had been, with the seating plan and Skills Class starting right away. Hali and her words! I wasn't sure what onerous meant, but it wasn't good. So I was working overtime cheering those two up. I myself wasn't thrilled with homework on the first day, even six words of it, so maybe I needed cheering, too.

We'd been best friends forever, but there were things I'd never told them. One was that I kind of liked Skills Class. We all loved Mr. Locke; he was the best. He was the one who thought learning a new word a day was so important, but of course, Hali was the only one who kept on with it. It was too ... onerous? ... for Faye and me.

Wow! I did it—a new word!

Mr. Locke knew and cared about us, and was always thinking of new ways for us to become the best we could be. Of course, he didn't know *everything* about us, but he knew enough. And if there was ever anyone we could tell the rest, it was Mr. Locke. But of course, we never would.

Plus, it was safe in SC. There was no one to pull a face if Hali didn't hear something, or edge away from Faye like she was contagious if she started hypering out. Not to mention me, wheezing and sneezing and all that.

At least, it used to be safe, with the three of us.

But now there were four.

Stazy

The house, when I got to it, looked dead. No Mom hauling in groceries or hunched over her laptop in the window. No Ryan dangling car keys, saying I'd made us late for parkour again. And of course, no Dad, doing anything at all.

It was weird to think Mom was working at that earthy-smelling garden store past the school. It was even weirder to think that this was the same neighbourhood she'd grown up in. She'd even gone to my new school! I hoped her first day had been a little easier than mine.

As I inched up the sidewalk, fumbling for my key, I noticed that compared to the other tidy lawns I'd passed, ours looked a little shaggy. A picture of Dad, mega-energized and flipping back that lock of black hair that loved to hang in his eyes as he scooted up and down with our old lawnmower, suddenly struck me. Who would mow the grass now? Mom? ME??

The key worked. Stale food smells—someone else's dinners—met me when I opened the door, and I was ready to go back out and sit on the porch untill Mom showed, when I heard a tiny meow from the kitchen.

How could I have forgotten? Carter appeared in the hall a second later, then thrust his back up into a kitten-shattering stretch. I picked up his perfect little furball self, and suddenly all that school stuff pushed off just a bit. Grumpy didn't stand a chance against that roaring purr in my ear.

Faye

The first "thing" I saw when I came in the door was Ginger, my twin.

All those books you read about how horrible it is to be a twin? All those movies you see about how wonderful it is to be a twin? Some days it was both, and some days it was neither. I had a feeling about which today would be.

"Hey! How was *your* first day?" I said. On the kitchen table in front of her were tidy piles of perfectly-sharpened pencils and pencil crayons, multi-coloured pens, and erasers she'd probably never need.

"Great! How about yours?" One of Ginger's eyes was focused on stocking the best-equipped pencil case Northridge School had ever seen; the other was checking out my pearls and sweater set. I wish I'd had a camera.

"Okay, sort of." I dropped my bag on the floor and grabbed an apple from a bowl on the counter. "I tried really hard to concentrate on what my teacher was saying, but my brain just skips around the room, goes out the window, replays a commercial I saw yesterday." As usual, we were in different classes; some twins were always put in the

12

same class, and some twins never were. For some reason, we were in the second group.

"Aw, Faye. Do you think you should go back to the medicine that Dr. Henshaw prescribed?" Ginger looked sympathetic, but then a poorly-sharpened pencil caught her eye. "Anyway, it'll be easier tomorrow, when the real work starts!" Grinding the pencil tip to perfection, she sounded completely pumped.

"Yeah, that'll be much better," I said, staring at her in amazement. We might share DNA, but there was nothing similar about our attitudes to school. Or medication, apparently. I opened the back door and stepped into the garden. From there, I moved past the lawn furniture and veggie beds to the back of our garden; quieter and wilder than the tidy patio area.

As soon as I was surrounded by the two giant cedars and clusters of chrysanthemums and dahlias, I could feel the stress of Day One easing off. I sat cross-legged at the base of one tree, leaning against its shaggy bark. In front of me, silvery water splashed down rocks into the pond; a wide-eyed frog hoisted itself from the murk onto a lily pad. A hummingbird whizzed past, and a pair of squirrels started down the trunk behind me, chattering.

I leaned back and closed my eyes, totally calm. Why couldn't I feel this way at school?

Hali

The house was chaos, as usual, when I got home. Barnston was in his room, but the door was vibrating with the sound of his tuba. You know you've lost the jackpot when your fourteen-year-old brother decides to take up the tuba. Evan and Clayton were fighting—again—with Guy. At six and seven, they seemed too old to have an imaginary friend, but if they had to have one, did they have to fight with him all the time?

The only upside to hearing aids was being able to shut them off when the going got tough, which was almost every time I stepped into my house. So I did. The tuba settled into a distant bleating, and the argument became arms waving and cheeks puffing, but only peeps of noise. Perfect.

Mom breezed by with an armload of sheets. She pressed her cheek to mine and said something. Luckily I'm a pretty good lip reader, 'cuz she doesn't like me shutting my aids off. Mom thinks it's disrespectful of my brothers and isolating for me, but she doesn't have to live with three amplified brothers, one amplifying imaginary friend, two super amp hearing aids, and a tuba.

Talk about onerous.

"It was fine, Mom." She'd asked about school. "Rena, Faye, and I are in the same class, probably 'cuz it's easier to cut us out of the pack in one class to go to Mr. Locke, but who cares why? At least we're together." I was about to mention that new girl—that black cape! Those black-and-orange tights! Combat boots! I mean, Rena and her Wild, Wild West outfits were one thing, but that girl brought a whole new meaning to the phrase "off-trend". But Mom was now asking Guy why he'd broken the head off her tap-dance trophy.

There was no use asking why she was speaking to an imaginary person, because I'd tried that lots of times. Obviously, I wasn't the only person who didn't hear well in this family.

Or listen.

Rena

To be honest, I was still feeling a little wheezy from the perfume the new girl, Stazy, had been wearing at school. I don't think she'd seen the *No Scent Zone* sign. I took one last gulp of air and tried to look relaxed and calm before I pushed open the front door. I was removing my shoes when one of my dads, Harlan, came down the hall.

"Rena! How was the first day of school?" Harlan is more enthusiastic than a mouse at a cheese convention. He is short and wiry and his hugs can leave you with broken bones. He held out his arms, and in I went.

I was feeling that air I'd gulped getting squeezed back out again when my other dad, Alex, appeared in the door to the kitchen. He had an apron around his kinda bulgy tummy, and his eyes were lively above his grey-striped beard.

"Come see! I've made you a special after-first-day-of-school snack," he said, ushering what was left of me from Harlan's hug into the kitchen. On the table were little bowls with olives and dips and little pieces of bread and . . . *mmmmm*. I don't know what it all was, but I dove in. Both my dads loved to cook, and it was a good thing because when you had as many allergies as me, it took a lot of time and energy to prepare food.

Harlan was nibbling an olive, testing a dip, while Alex grabbed the biggest piece of bread he could find and piled it with some of everything. Harlan took one long look at the bread, then another at Alex's tummy, but Alex just smiled and picked some dip out of his beard.

Alex was pointing at the bowls, saying "gluten-free bread" and "organic olives" and a bunch of other things. I nodded and kept eating, but my head was back at school. What a day! A coughing fit the first day, the new girl and those tights and that perfume, a brand new western outfit, and a six-word assignment.

It was enough to make you say doggone it, doggone it, doggone it (hey . . . that's six words!) and eat more olives. And cough a bit.

Faye

Carrie, Mom's office assistant, called to say that Mom was behind with her patients, but that there was a casserole in the freezer and she'd be home by eight. She said something else, too, but as she talked, I started getting that itchy gotta-move feeling. I bounced past the gauzy curtains and green velvet couches in the living room and into the sunroom, its walls covered in jewel-tone butterflies. I felt so hyper that I stuck a couple of fingers into the fountain burbling there. As always, the water helped.

She was still talking when I came to a dead stop in front of the hall mirror. I was so used to the faun holding the mirror, its lower half a goat, its upper half a human with little goat horns on top, that it hardly even registered. Didn't everyone have mirrors like this? I guess our house was kind of a clue about us, but to me, it seemed one-hundred percent regular.

It was what was in the mirror that concerned me. My sweater set was buttoned wrong and my new bob looked like someone had poured glue on it and then hung me upside down for a week. The green streaks in my hair were way more obvious than they'd been this morning when I sprayed them into submission. And worse than that, my ears, with those interesting almost-points on the top, were showing! I was very glad to see that the pearls were still there, so when Carrie finally felt she'd micromanaged every possible dinner detail, I said goodbye and carefully undid the clasp. I slipped the necklace back in its place in Mom's room, behind her bedroom fountain. I hadn't even lost it! That made my "borrowing" only minor mischief!

Then I went into the room Ginger and I shared—one half as if a cleaning team had just left, the other half as if a hurricane had done the same. I found my sweats under the bed and a t-shirt I was using as a bookmark. I exchanged it for the sweater set, noticed with satisfaction that water from our bedroom fountain was dripping slightly onto Ginger's pillow, and went back to the kitchen to find the casserole.

In Mom's neat-and-tidy freezer compartment, it was easy to find dinner, labelled "Veg Casserole". Since Mom, Ginger, and I were all vegetarians, I wasn't sure why it needed the word "veg" there, but that was Mom—organized, methodical, meticulous.

Like Ginger, I thought as I pulled the casserole out and headed toward the microwave. Two steps later, the frozen mass slipped from my hands and landed on my left foot. I leapt around for a few minutes, screeching and wailing.

Limping, I plunked the dented dish into the microwave. Yes, like Ginger, I thought again. Not so much like me.

Stazy

I was explaining the six-word thing to Carter—oh come on! Everyone talks to their cat!—when the door pushed open and there was Mom. After her long days of writing, I was used to Mom Exhaustion in the form of semi-bloodshot eyes accompanied by two hands to the back, wincing and creaking as she tried to straighten up. The garden store version involved more rubbing of the forehead—headache?—and dirt. Definitely more dirt.

After she had scrubbed her hands with soap and more soap, she turned to me, gave me a hug and asked about dinner.

Dinner?" I asked. You mean the meal that appears effortlessly at the end of the day? Luckily that part wasn't out loud.

"Staz . . . I am now working eight hours a day, five days a week. You'll be home two hours before me. Sometimes you're going to have to help me out." She caught sight of her laptop, and her shoulders drooped even further. "Especially since I'll only have nights and weekends to write."

She looked so tired that I forced a small "Okay, Mom," out of my mouth. But it wasn't easy. What I wanted to say was that if she hadn't made Dad leave, she wouldn't have to be choosing potted plants over literary fame. And we wouldn't have had to move to this weenie house and . . . I didn't even want to think about school.

We settled for mac and cheese. I rummaged through the fridge until I found some leftover sliced ham. It's not really a meal unless there's meat in it, right? We took our bowls outside and sat on the back steps. Mom was so keen to have a first-day-of-school celebration that she even let me have pop with dinner. "But just for tonight, Staz. We're going to drink milk, and eat at the table, and have proper dinners starting tomorrow, just like before." I heard the words she *wasn't* saying just as well as the words she was—that she and I on our own were just as much a family as the four of us had been. I didn't agree, but obviously I didn't get a vote. With Ryan away in his first year of university and Dad in that little apartment on the other side of the city, it was just Mom and me. And luckily, Carter.

I knew there'd be nights when we'd have to negotiate for the laptop, what with Mom writing and me doing homework, but I figured that tonight, I could handwrite six words without too much trauma. Mom writes fantasy novels, very long books that take a lot of time to write but don't pay enough for groceries. She definitely couldn't handwrite.

So we settled in the tiny living room, Mom and her laptop on the couch, me and my scrap of paper by the window.

"*Hmmmmmm,*" she said, starting out with a long yawn.

"*Hmmmm,*" I said, joining in.

Then she started tapping away, like someone had fired a starter pistol. My little scrap stayed blank.

Hali

Six words for the whole summer? The only six that kept coming to mind were *Shut up downstairs! I can't think!* It was your average night at the Jordan Zoo. The animals had been fed and watered, but were on a rampage until the keepers locked them in their cages for the night.

I looked around my room for inspiration. At first glance, the most inspiring thing was the lock on the bedroom door. I'd had to campaign for weeks for that, but finally Mom caved when Guy and the terrors came in uninvited and left Glockenspiel, my turtle, crawling around on the floor. I hesitated to use the word again, so looked up a synonym for "onerous". The turtle situation had been extremely vexatious.

I was certainly inspired by all the amazing seashore scenes I had tacked up on every available wall in my room: Greek islands, Hawaiian beaches, surfers, whales, and coral reefs bursting with a rainbow of fish. Instinctively, I felt for the seashell I always kept on my night table. Cream-coloured with brown speckles, it was ridged and bumpy with a wide opening. Inside that, ocean waves crashed when I held it to my ear. It was a gift from my dad the day I got my hearing aids, and although I needed my aids to hear, it seemed to me that I needed my shell to exist.

Holding the shell, I took another long look at my beachy walls. Looking at pictures was the best I could do because I certainly never got to any of those places. Once again, this summer, the Jordans had spent their holiday dollars on a cabin in the mountains. The Jordans did mountains and deserts and farms; the Jordans did not, not ever, do oceans. I knew why, and it was *not* inspiring. So I kept thinking.

I caught a glimpse of myself in the mirror across from my desk, and inched over so I could get a better look. The muscles I'd developed from a lifetime of running were inspiring, and so were the waist length wavy red hair and greeny-blue eyes. I was even learning to like my paler-than-milk skin, but had a way to go on the army of freckles that plastered my nose.

The house was finally getting quiet. It was almost lights out time in the monkey habitat. I held my hair up and checked the mirror, then tried it in a ponytail. I practised smiling showing all my teeth, and then close-mouthed, looking mysterious and mature.

I looked out the window, where a beachless but beautiful sunset was performing, and finally, I began to write.

Rena

"Wow—six words. Only six words," Harlan murmured. His endless energy seemed zapped by the word restriction.

"You did so much. Gospel choir camp! The Claremont Western Film Festival!" said Alex.

"A hundred and fifty-nine trips to the animal shelter to convince us to get a dog," Harlan continued, then winced. "*Oooh*, I take that back."

Alex nodded and tugged on his beard. "Yup, probably better to let sleeping dogs lie." Harlan and I both groaned on cue; Alex beamed as if we'd clapped.

"Those were all great, Dad Unit, but you're missing the real highlight."

"No. Really?" Alex said.

"Well, I didn't want to mention it in case you felt obliged, but now that you've brought it up . . . " Harlan reached up and hung his arm around Alex's neck.

The wedding! My dads had finally gotten married this summer. They had waited forever, until the laws changed to allow same-sex marriage where we live, but *zam*! Once that happened, they were ready with peony floral arrangements, appetizers that had guests begging for recipes, and a solo by yours truly. There was a very large wedding portrait in the living room of Alex and Harlan, dressed to kill, gazing at me in adoration as I belted out their tune. As usual, I looked too skinny, but my white-blonde hair was for once curled and gelled into submission, instead of sticking out at many strange angles. Also as usual, my brown eyes looked too huge and too puppy-doggish for a human face. But that made sense, right?

"Of course that was the highlight! Now if you two will let me concentrate, I'll find the exact six words to make Ms. Burnside scream in rapture." They rose as one from the couch in the den, from where they'd been cheerleading. "Don't think I've forgotten about the dog," I called as they were closing the door. "One battle at a time!"

Just for a second after the door closed, I thought about another part of my summer: all the time I'd spent stuffed up with allergies, the trips to the doctor's for shots, and the day my asthma had kicked into overdrive and I'd ended up in Emergency. I shook my head to clear it, then grabbed a pen.

Faye

I tried to get Ginger to write my six words. No luck. I thought of a few, but none seemed quite right. *Smart twin refuses to help dummy. Help your local kid. Ban September.* I was almost enjoying myself, until Hali sent me a text to remind me that the topic was something significant from our summer. As usual, I was off topic.

When I heard Mom downstairs, finally home from work, I flicked off my light and went down. I was obviously concentrating too hard; I'd just let the words find *me,* instead of chasing after them.

That oughta work.

Faye

Walking to school with Rena and Hali. Still no words. I must be hard to find.

Stazy

"New life: my starter is Carter." I blurted it out when it was my turn. Ms. Burnside said we didn't have to explain it, but that others could ask questions, if they wanted. I was pretty sure no one would ask the new kid anything. And I was almost right.

The cowboy girl put up her hand. Maybe she was mad that I'd worn the perfume yesterday? Or grateful that I hadn't today? The teacher called her Serene, but yesterday I'd heard her friends call her Rena.

"So . . . who's Carter?" Today she had on a black shirt with white embroidery all over the place and—surprise!—fringes. But her face didn't look mean; she just wanted to know.

"He's my kitten. I got him a couple of days ago, when I moved into the new house." She was nodding and smiling; that was good enough for me. As I sat down, I made sure I didn't look around at anyone else, in case they weren't looking as friendly.

Rena went next. She stood up and glanced quickly at the red-haired one, then said, "Sang two hearts together. Heavenly bliss!" She waited one half-second for questions, then sank into her seat.

I had to sneak a peek at her—at Hali, even though I didn't know her name then. I didn't know what Rena had been looking for, but what was there was a pair of high eyebrows and bugged-out eyes, quickly replaced by a tight little smile and a glance over at the one with the greenish hair. That one was staring at a piece of paper in her hand. No pearls today, and quite a different look, actually. That's when

21

I noticed the bumblebee again, floating over her head. What kind of a crazy classroom was this?

Hali

Was she crazy? Here we were, trying to fit in, and Rena practically pointed a sign toward one of the parts of her life that made her so different! "Heavenly bliss!" What was she thinking??

When it was my turn, I stood up tall and said the words, "Ran fast. Had to! Three brothers." Everyone laughed, which was just what I wanted. I knew it was good, and that Ms. Burnside would like it. It told about part of me, but not the part that I didn't want people to know about. Unlike Rena!

I didn't hear which name Ms. Burnside said next, but I could tell it was Faye. She grabbed the piece of paper in her hand. I was close enough to be able to see that it was blank. She looked at Rena, then at me, then stood up. She looked down at the paper, then out the window, where summer was still hanging on, teasing us. Then she opened her mouth.

"Sunshine. Leaves. Dance of the bumblebee."

I put my head on my desk. First Rena. Now Faye. Our secrets! I took a humungous, calming breath. Calm. Calm. After all, no one could even see the bumblebee. Calm. Calm.

Ms. Burnside was bubbling volcanically, giving Faye the thumbs-up, babbling about the cadence of her words. Faye looked ecstatic; this might be the only time all year she was class star.

Calm.

Faye

"I just made it up on the spot!" I told Mr. Locke. "I looked out the window, and there were leaves and sunshine and . . . "

"Bumblebees? You saw bumblebees?"

I didn't even have to look at Hali or Rena. I knew the answer to this one.

"Yeah, I did. I saw one bumblebee."

"That's fantastic, Faye, and so is your poem. Congratulations!"

Stazy was smiling at me, just a small not-taking-too-much-of-a-chance smile. I gave her back pretty much the same kind of smile.

Mr. Locke continued. "I've just decided on today's word: serendipitous. It's serendipitous that Faye looked out the window just then, that the scene reminded her of some important elements of her summer." He leaned toward me and looked me seriously in the eye. "It's serendipitous that she is a person who can create lovely poems on the spot." The bell went, and we all started to collect our backpacks.

"But next time, Faye," he called as we pushed out the door, "don't count on serendipity. Get your homework done, all right?"

He had a point.

Stazy

It was *not* serendipitous that I found myself walking home behind those girls again.

Hali seemed to be doing most of the talking. Her arms were waving, her hair was floating behind her as if a wind had whipped crimson fall leaves into a cape. The other two were nodding, and after a bit, there was a lot of laughing, from all three.

I kept my eyes on my shoes, sneaking glances now and then to make sure I didn't walk my striped legs into a car or a cowgirl.

But that evening, after we ate my first attempt at spaghetti (quite horrible!), my grandmother called. Mom's voice was stiff and bristly as she spoke, so I knew it was either Dad or Abuelita.

After they talked for a few minutes, Mom passed the phone to me. My chat with Abuelita was short, but it left me bursting. "She wants me to come for the weekend!" I told Mom after I'd hung up.

"I know, Stazy." Her voice was all funny.

"Well . . . I can go, right?"

"I don't know, love." She looked confused, but I couldn't believe it wasn't just a simple 'yes'. I could feel everything—new school with no friends, new lonely house, everything!—rolling into an angry black ball.

"Mom, I don't have my friends or my house or mostly, my Dad. You can't do this!"

She looked like she wanted to.

"She's my grandmother! You can't take her, too!"

All she said was, "I know she is, Stazy. But she's something else, too." And there it was, this whole problem for me, my parents, my brother. How would we ever get past this horrible, wonderful secret?

I wanted to slam a door, or at least flounce out like they do on TV, as if there's a point to it. But for us, this was at the core of everything, and no flouncing or slamming would change it. Besides, our kitchen only had the back door, and if I flounced out of it, where was I going to go then?

We stood, looking at each other, until Mom came and wrapped her arms around me and said, "Yes, go. She *is* your grandmother."

All my mad trickled out. Why couldn't it always be like this? I hugged her back, and it felt good.

I just wished I could wipe away the little frown line down the middle of Mom's forehead, the one that said she still wasn't sure it was the right thing to do.

Rena

Friday afternoon, last period. Skills Class.

Buzzzzzz. The bee was making lazy circles over Faye's head, and I could relate. My brain was definitely buzzy, and if I felt any lazier, my eyes would shut completely, instead of half way, as they were. Even with the windows open, Mr. Locke's room was baking hot. I was beginning to agree with Hali; maybe a fringed leather skirt in September *wasn't* the best idea.

There was also something—I couldn't tell what: blossoming or floating or some other annoying thing—that was tickling away at my allergies, and my nose was getting stuffy, that itchy feeling in my eyes. I was allergic to so many things that I was used to it; half the time I couldn't even tell what I was reacting to. Some people might think it was weird that Hali and I were even in the Skills Class. Allergies? Hearing loss? But we both missed a lot—Hali because of her hearing, and me, because I was forever away with asthma, allergies, or busy catching whatever bug was being generously shared around our class. So the extra help, helped.

"Girls, we're all half asleep here!" Mr. Locke said. Not only was he an amazing teacher, he was psychic! Or had I been snoring?

"Ten minutes left. Let's put away the books and each of you tell me what you're doing this weekend. I want a detailed, interesting account, not a list. Hali, you first!"

Mr. Locke didn't usually call on Hali first, because of her ears. Hali didn't always ask if she hadn't heard something, because it happened a lot. So it was better for her to go second or third, after she had a better idea of what was going on. But Mr. Locke wasn't the Skills Teacher for nothing; I could see that he'd been speaking carefully in Hali's direction, and he could tell that she had understood and was ready to go.

"I'm training for a 10K race next month," she started. "I'm doing a long run tomorrow morning, and then I'm . . . " she stopped here, looking up at the board where today's word was written, ". . . *dismayed* to be babysitting my two little brothers . . . and their friend." She described the running and brother horror a bit more, mindful of Mr. Locke's instructions. Hali tried to make up for her hearing by doing everything else perfectly at school. As far as I could see, she was totally crushing it.

Faye was volunteering at the animal shelter and planting some bulbs for spring with her mom. Of course, we three were hanging out, but it didn't seem right to say that in front of Stazy. I kind of wished she could come along.

Faye

Eight minutes to three. Seven minutes to three. I realized I was tapping my pencil against the desk. Why were some minutes so much longer than others?

Next came Stazy. I hadn't paid much attention to her that week; too busy with pearls, sweatpants, and avoiding homework, I guess. She kept to herself and seemed to like looking at the floor a lot.

I saw Rena smiling at her when she thought Hali and I didn't see, which I didn't get. I mean, did she think we'd tell her not to? Me? Hali?

Well, Hali. Maybe Rena was right. Hali might tell her not to. She had had a couple of things to say about Stazy's outfits, that was for sure. I glanced over at Hali; as usual, she looked amazing. She was wearing greeny-blue shorts and a shimmery turquoise t-shirt. Were those little shells tied in her hair? If anyone else did that, they'd look ridiculous; with Hali, it looked great. Even more than running, even more than her pet turtle, Hali *loved* the ocean, and it usually showed in her clothes.

Stazy's turn. Eyes on the floor, she started. "I'm staying with my *abuelita* this weekend. That's what I call my grandmother; she's from Mexico." She lifted her eyes to Mr. Locke, who nodded and smiled, encouraging her on.

"I love hanging out with her because she's unusual, in a fun way, I mean, and she makes me all kinds of great Mexican food. And . . . we have the same hobby."

Mr. Locke hadn't asked anyone else questions, but this was more words than had come out of Stazy's mouth all week, so he probably wanted to keep her going. "And what is the hobby, Stazy? Music? Painting?"

"No." Stazy was halfway sitting down now, and she had a look that said, "Woops. Why did I say that?" on her face. But she answered, "Magic," and then plopped into her chair.

"Magic." Mr. Locke nodded his head, thinking that one over. "Magic," he said again. "Very interesting, Stazy."

Rena was last. She launched in, so Rena-like, excited about watching a Wild-West film festival with Harlan and Alex, and an extra-long choir practice with her gospel group for a concert that was coming up. Rena sang because she loved it, but also because her dads thought it was a good way to strengthen her lungs. When she wasn't wheezing, she had a really good voice.

I loved watching her talk. She was like a little kid, Rena. She got so excited that sometimes she smacked her hands together, and her brown eyes were sparkling. But then I noticed that not everyone was watching her.

Stazy's eyes were somewhere else—they were making lazy circles over my head, watching something moving above. I looked up, even though I knew what it was. I looked up, really slowly. Because I knew that once I was totally sure what was up there, and that Stazy could see it, everything would be different.

Yup. It was my bee. The bee that only Hali and Rena and I could see. It had been there most of the week—bees love crazy hot weather!—but Mr. Locke had never seen it, or Ms. Burnside, or any of the other kids. If you could see my bee, you were . . . special, like us three. Not the Special that got you into Skills Class, but another kind of special.

I stared so hard at Hali that she eventually looked at me. Once I had her attention, I looked over at Stazy, who was still checking out my bee, and then I lifted my eyes up above me, where the bee was motoring around. Hali's eyes followed mine, and then opened very wide.

Rena sat down. The bell rang.

This changed everything.

Part 2

First Weekend

Stazy

At last, the weekend. I raced home, dropped some cat food in Carter's dish and cuddled him goodbye. Then I grabbed the duffel bag I'd packed earlier. Mom wouldn't be home for a while, but she knew I was busing to Abuelita's. That morning, she'd given me ten dollars for bus fare and spending money, and ten million warnings about safety, manners, weather, and global warming. Okay, maybe not the last one, but she was thorough!

I *was* a little nervous, 'cuz the whole bus thing was new for me. Before Mom and Dad split up, we had a car, and most places I needed to get to, I got a ride. Now, with Mom working and me going to school walking distance from our house, the car was a luxury Mom said we couldn't afford.

But I knew the route, and called Mom when I got to the bus stop, with a promise to call again when I was at Abuelita's. I watched the street signs, rang the buzzer at the right one, and caught the connecting bus. It was a snap! An hour later, I was outside the apartment. I called Mom and then pushed the buzzer.

"Anastasia? Is that you?" Abuelita did something with my name that no one else in the world could get close to. Following the Grandmother's Handbook, she used my full name, but she also rolled the 'z' sound and made all the 'a' sounds exactly the same. I didn't like my full name much, but when Abuelita said it, it sounded perfect.

Of course she'd made my favourite Mexican dish, chicken *chimis*, and the smell was leaking out of her tiny kitchen right into my nose. Her apartment was just like her: organized chaos. There were too many books, plants, and knick-knacks to look tidy, but she could find anything in a second. She was wearing jeans and a cherry-red shirt that made her cheeks bloom; a few grey strands escaped the mostly-black braid over her shoulder.

She hugged me so hard that we both started to laugh, then sent me down the hall to my room. It was really her workroom, but when I stayed the night, she always set it up just for me. I hesitated before opening the door to the room; could this, like everything else in my life, have changed, too? But no. When I peeked in, the bed was covered with a multicoloured blanket, my favourite kids' books lined the shelves, and the little lamp on the bedside table cast a yellowy pool of light in the soft darkness.

The *chimis* were calling me from the kitchen, but I sat down on the bed anyway, calm settling over me. This was a safe place. If only Mom could see that. But I knew what Mom saw at Abuelita's now: creepiness and evil. How could I change her mind?

I settled back against the pillows for a second, and I think I must have been almost asleep when Abuelita came to the door.

"*Chimis* are ready. How about you?" She was looking at me closely, maybe asking about more than just food?

Yes. Definitely, yes.

Hali

Saturday morning. Running.

By the time I reached the lake, I was running hard but hardly puffing at all.

There was always that stretch at the beginning where my breath had to work to keep up with my legs, but soon I was floating along, my feet barely seeming to touch the ground, my arms pumping along in time, breathing easy. My body could go flying by the lake without a second thought, but my head never could. So I aimed for a grassy space just up from the sand and let myself flop on my back.

I lay as I'd landed for a few moments, my head faced away from the water. But it was as if the waves whispered, coaxing my eyes to find them. So I flipped belly down, chin resting on my fists, eyes resting on the water. It was, after all, the reason this was my running route.

The air was warm, but there was a breeze that pushed little waves back and forth, the sun glinting here and there off their crests. It was a perfect day. Birds were darting about in the trees; I couldn't exactly hear their song, but I had a pretty good idea of how it might sound. I knew the water would be cool already, even though it was only early September. Summer's heat usually faded as soon as August was out of sight. Still, I wanted to be in that water, as always.

Ripping off my socks and runners, I stuck my feet in and yikes! It *was* cold. But my feet felt so good. I went in a little farther, so my calves could feel that caress, too. And I wanted to go farther and farther and farther.

But, I didn't. As Mom and Dad always said, the Jordans weren't swimmers. We were runners and tap dancers and soccer players and tuba players, but not swimmers. I'd never had a single swimming lesson, partly because being in the water meant taking out my hearing aids, and not being able to use my hearing aids to hear the instructions before entering the water would have made it impossible. But we all knew that was only the smallest part of the reason. The other part was why this water, even lake water, called out to me in large, loud capital letters to dive in and swim, swim, swim.

So I just looked at it, and it just looked at me. Eventually the soul-destroying thought that it was almost time to babysit my brothers entered my watery brain, so I dried my feet off as best I could and stuffed them back into my socks and runners. They weren't too happy, and neither was I.

I guess it's good to be attuned to your feet. Attuned: another one of Mr. Locke's words.

Rena

"No, no, people! Have another look at the music, please. This part is loud, forte! You sound about as loud and energy-filled as Santa's workshop the day after Christmas."

Wow. Just think about that. How quiet and wiped-out all those elves would be. Maybe just laying back and sipping . . . oh, we'd started the song again, and I was worrying about elf cocoa.

I jumped back in. Easy-peasy! I was one of the best sight readers in the choir, so I glanced at the music and then let my voice float back up into the high soprano line. Sometimes it was almost too easy, so I had to make sure I listened to instructions about breathing correctly and using my diaphragm to get the best out of my voice. But even when I didn't do it, my voice found those high notes and danced around up there like a butterfly amongst hot summer flowers, exactly where it was supposed to be. The song ended. Jazmine, our director, had a few more things to say.

Hot summer flowers. *Oooh*, bad image. Pollen and sneezing and itchy eyes. Think about something else!

"This part needs to be sung sharp and distinct. Syncopated," Jazmine said. Her frizzy hair bounced as she emphasized the way she wanted us to sing. I got it. She kept going, describing how we'd be doing it. My mind wiggled away, back to where it seemed to want to rest lately.

Stazy, the new girl. How nervous and unhappy she'd seemed all week, until the moment in Skills Class when she'd talked about her grandmother—was it *aboola*, she'd called her?—and her plans for the weekend. I had been feeling that other energy, the sad stuff, just rolling off her, and I felt it roll right away when she got going about the good food she'd be having and—yeah! She'd said magic, that's what they did together.

That was kind of strange. What could she know about magic? Probably rabbits in hats and long handkerchiefs pulled out of sleeves. Probably. My mind kept coming back to her, over and over.

There was something about that Stazy. Her sadness made me sad, but it was more than that. I was just deciding that I'd have to find out what it was, when I heard, "Rena? Did your body just join us today and leave your mind and voice elsewhere?"

Aaaaghhhh. I chased Stazy back into a corner and opened my mouth to sing.

Faye

ADHD was no fun. Saying or spelling it out in full—attention deficit hyperactivity disorder—was bad, but not nearly as bad as having it. It was hard for me to sit still and listen in class. My mind often snagged on something else and got stuck there, instead of steering back to nouns and verbs and decimal places. I'd tried some pills to help with it, but I hated them. I felt so . . . calm. All the time. Even when a dog walker went by with dogs yipping and yelping at me; calm. When Hali and Rena knocked on my door with a frog-and-lily-pad shaped birthday cake; calm. So bye-bye pills!

Mom and I worked on strategies to help me focus. I got lots of exercise, lots of sleep, lots of days where the closest thing I came to screen time was operating the microwave. I think it helped.

So here we were, spending time in the great outdoors. I don't even know why I said it like that because I loved being outside. I guess I got tired of being on a program, always focusing on focusing, if you know what I mean.

Anyway, we were planting bulbs in the back garden. Mom was methodically spading up dirt, tucking in bulbs and re-covering each one. Her plantings were tidy yet inspired, just like her. She was logical and practical—like Ginger—but crazily creative, too. I guess I fit the role of the crazily creative twin, but maybe the emphasis was on the crazy part.

My plantings were a little haphazard. So maybe we needed a daffodil or two sprouting beside the compost bin? I watched Mom carefully for a minute, trying to pick up pointers. Her straight, black hair swung around her jaw as she worked, her almond-shaped eyes never strayed from her latest digging spot.

I don't know why I needed to, but once again, I checked her ring finger. Dad died when I was five, which seemed forever ago, but somehow I still wanted her to keep wearing that wedding ring. Forever.

It was there, along with a teardrop blue ring from a cousin in China. Typically, although her hands were working with dirt, her rings and nails looked perfect. I looked down at mine. What a mess.

I started digging again, then noticed my bee swirling lazily above me, playing around in the heat that would disappear any day. My fingers kept digging, but my mind shot back to Stazy's eyes in Skills Class yesterday, watching the bee. When I finally had a chance to talk to Hali about it, she said she thought it was just a fluke, that Stazy hadn't really been able to see it. Hali used the voice she pulls out when she wants her will to be enough to make something so, and it usually works. Usually.

But I'd seen Stazy's eyes, absentmindedly rolling around as she focused on the air above my head.

"Faye! Are you intending to plant that bulb in this country, or is it for one of our Chinese relatives?" I jerked back to bulbs and Mom and a very, very big hole.

I left Stazy and Hali and the bee behind as I dropped dirt back into the hole. Mom was great. Most of the time she never even said the dreaded word, "focus", but I knew she was thinking it.

So was I. When I could focus, that is.

Stazy

Waking up at Abuelita's place was heaven. Something involving bacon was being fried up in the kitchen. My room was completely familiar and Abuelita was singing loudly in Spanish. No worries, no frowns, no watchful glances to see how I was doing.

And I absolutely loved bacon. And steak. And hamburger. And chicken. I was very . . . meaty. I'd had vegetarian friends who carefully explained about animal rights and the horrible lives of a lot of farmed animals; I understood and felt a little guilty, but there was nothing more delicious than a slice—well, many slices—of bacon crunch-

crunching between my teeth, or the first bite of a juicy hamburger. I was guilty, but I was meaty. Mom said that meat gave me lots of energy for parkour, and I guess she was right about that, but Abuelita said it was our heritage because she loved eating meat, too.

I slipped from under the covers and out into the hall. From there, I could see into the kitchen, and the loud singing was even louder. I hadn't learned much Spanish—it was one of the things I was hoping Abuelita would teach me more of—but I could tell that the song was about either a donkey, a car accident, or a bag of donuts.

I watched Abuelita cooking. She was expertly flipping strips of bacon with one hand and scooping eggs around in a second pan with the other. She kept looking over at the toaster, checking to see when it would pop. I could see my orange juice glass already on the table, and I knew her coffee must be nearby. Abuelita didn't function that well in the morning without her coffee; in fact, she hardly functioned at all.

She was still flipping and scooping and toast-eyeballing when something indigo-coloured on the counter near her snagged my eye. I noticed it because it seemed to shift forward just a little. Then it stopped. Then it moved ahead again. It was Abuelita's cup.

I watched as it started moving again, now gliding smoothly to the edge of the counter. Then it launched itself into the air. It sailed itself right up to Abuelita. Her hands still cooking, she shifted her eyes away from the toaster to gauge the distance between her cup and her mouth, and when it was close enough, dipped in to grab a nice long slurp as the cup tilted obligingly forward.

She did love her coffee.

Faye

On Saturday at noon, we met at the library. Me, Rena, and Hali. Not my idea, that's for sure. But Hali said it would be good to get into the habit. "It's important to set our habits right from the start," she said, flipping her red waterfall of hair behind her. "We don't have any projects yet, but we will soon. Let's be proactive. Right?"

That Hali. What a crazy idea. Easy for her and Rena! They both loved books, and could spend hours with their heads hanging into open pages, gobbling up whatever food it is they were getting out of there. Me? Well, I *liked* books. I liked them after I'd been walking in the woods for hours, so my *jumpies* were all jumped out. I liked them after a soccer game, or after recess, when I could flop onto my chair behind my desk, and Ms. Burnside started the next chapter of our class read aloud. But on Sunday afternoon, when we could be watching something good on TV and stuffing in some cheese balls or chips and dip? At the library it was water only, to protect the books. I guess they didn't want cheese-ball fingerprints on every page; I got that.

And I got that the hang-out-at-the-library plan was for me. When the projects came, Hali and Rena would have no problem getting their work done; this was their latest plan to outsmart my ADHD and turn me into a scholar.

Hah. Fat chance.

But I loved Hali and Rena as much as they loved books—and me!—so of course I went.

Rena

It wasn't that my book wasn't doggone amazing. It was! I was halfway through it, and I'd loved it from the moment I'd cracked it open. It was about a girl who did volunteer work at a hospital, and her supervisor didn't like her, and her brother was a bully, and her best friend had an eating problem. All that was fine, but the part I loved was her hospital work because I absolutely knew I'd be a doctor when I grew up.

I pushed back in my chair and let myself drift into a Dr. Rena daydream. There I was, listening with my stethoscope to a little boy's chest. I could hear his raggedy breathing—asthma and allergies again, like me. I knew just what to do: I had an exercise plan for him, ideas about making his house more breather-friendly, some medication, maybe. Here he was, back in a few months, breathing steady and even. I was an uber-doctor, a champion of the breathless, queen of the stethoscope.

Just then, I had a coughing fit. Dust! In between hacks, I looked for the source. There was Faye, an ancient book in her hands. I tried to catch a glimpse of the title, but another spaz of coughing got me. What did it matter? She wasn't reading it, just slowly opening and closing all those dusty pages, pumping out little clouds of dust in my direction.

Both Hali and Faye looked over at me, probably ready to run for water or pound me on the back if it looked like I needed it, but I tried to indicate with my now-runny eyes that I was going to be fine. Hali slid back into her book—something about an Olympic swimmer, I could see—and Faye opened the dust book and stared into it, eyes glazed.

My concentration was shot, and besides, I needed to walk around a bit and get some air. So I headed away from the deep cushions of the YA area and wandered into the non-fiction section. I was in pretty foreign territory there, but moving felt good, so I let my feet take charge.

Here were books about cooking—I wondered if my dads had the one about dairy-free desserts, 'cuz the cover looked amazing—books about paper folding and sculpture and . . . magic. Books about magic.

Why did I look around carefully before I bent down to pull out one of the magic books? I leaned back against the shelf, keeping one eye on the YA area while I flipped through instructions on pulling coins from behind your ear and doing clever things with a deck of cards. At first it looked pretty hokey, but after a couple minutes, I forgot about the YA area altogether. I eased into a nearby chair, eyes glued onto details about cutting a rope in half, then presenting the audience with a whole rope again. Well, it seemed like a whole rope. How did they do that?

I was rereading, moving my hands around to imitate the instructions in the book, when I heard, "Magic, Rena? Really?"

They were both standing there watching me, Hali still clutching her book, Faye's no doubt long forgotten. Faye's eyebrows were raised and Hali's were practically flying off her forehead.

I didn't know what to say. It wasn't about the book, of course. It was about why I'd been peeking back to where they were sitting when I walked over, until I "magically" got involved in the book and forgot to look.

It was about Stazy. It was about why I felt so drawn to her, and why Hali was so set on keeping her separate. It was about what made us different, about one of the things that cemented us as friends, a place where Stazy could never go.

Well, that's what we thought at the time.

I felt all prickly behind my neck and my stomach was doing back springs. Part of me wanted to drop the book and link arms with them, sail out of the blasted non-fiction section and go buy jelly beans at the market. I'm all about harmony. But another part wanted that book, *really* wanted that book and knew that it was somehow important to have it.

Besides, what was the big deal? It was just a book, right? I put it on a table.

"Yes, ma'am. Magic! I was studyin' up on some tricks to dazzle you with." Faye looked half-interested until she noticed that Hali was still in frown mode.

"Why magic? I didn't know you were interested in that."

Faye's eyes strayed over the open pages of the book, working the trick out. "Didn't the new girl say she was into magic? Is that what made you think of it?"

Hali's eyes were like a hawk; I hated feeling like a shivering mouse with my best friends.

"I guess it was, Faye. It just looked like . . ." I needed to say what I thought, tell Hali and Faye that there was nothing wrong with being friendly with Stazy. She was new and lonely and sure knew how to put together an interesting clothing look! Nothing as cool as cowboy boots and fringe, but I didn't want everyone wearing the same stuff as me, did I?

Instead, my prickly neck and springy stomach made me say, ". . . fun. It looked like fun." Hali, not impressed. Work on Faye. "Is it jelly bean time, yet? I'm starving!" Faye's eyes snapped open and she immediately started to move in the direction of the exit.

"It's totally time!" she called back, too loud for a library.

I smiled at Hali, and after a moment, she smiled back and started searching her jean pockets for her library card. As she headed toward the check-out desk, I quietly grabbed the magic book off the table and found my own card.

Stazy

Breakfast was awesome. As I gurgled down the end of my orange juice, Abuelita finished her coffee. Then she plunked her indigo cup on the table and said that after we cleared away the dishes, she'd work on a job she needed to do while I did my homework.

Wait, wait, wait. Back to that cup. You're thinking about the cup, right?

I think I need to say something now. Something about the cup. Yup, the cup and the coffee and Abuelita. And me.

We're kind of unusual, me and her. Well, her more than me. I'm working on being more unusual. My dad is unusual because he turned out to be so un-unusual.

I just reread that. Mumbo-jumbo, hocus-pocus, all of it. Which is pretty funny, considering what I'm about to say.

It was about six months ago, on a day that seemed like other days. I was visiting Abuelita, and she was cooking up a storm making us a bunch of great Mexican stuff for dinner. I'd helped for a while, then she told me to take a breather. The kitchen was a disaster, which is Abuelita's style. I was ready to escape the mess, so I went into the living room, pulled a random book off a shelf and flipped it open. Whatever possessed me? So out of character, I know.

But this book was different. Instead of the letters jumping and jiving here, there, and everywhere like they usually do, the words in this book stayed completely still, letting me read easily, encouraging me to read on and on and on. It was the first time I could ever remember a book that seemed Stazy-friendly. The reason for that, the reason for being in Skills Class—I'm dyslexic. That means that reading is a nightmare for me. The letters don't stay in one place when I'm looking at them, so it's hard to recognize words I've seen before and figure out ones I haven't. It makes reading faster than a slug crawls pretty impossible, too.

To me, the book seemed like a collection of recipes, but with a *craaazy* list of ingredients. For some of them you needed things like purple blooms harvested at midnight or an eagle feather drenched in morning dew. Some of the ingredients were a little more modern, like the first used cartridge from a new printer. After a couple of pages, I knew I wasn't looking at a cookbook. I knew what it wasn't, but I didn't know what it was.

Although the back of my neck was starting to feel all tingly, I had to keep reading. Some of the pages didn't have a list of ingredients at all. Instead, there were only directions. I remember one said something about stretching your arms toward the morning sun and repeating some words, opening and closing your eyes after each phrase. There was another one with some humming and then whispering certain letters. Most of the time I was so excited to actually be able to read it all so easily, that I was hardly concentrating on what anything meant.

But then I came to one without ingredients, and I started to read the directions and try to follow them exactly. I guess the thrill of reading was settling down a bit, and I was getting curious about what the pages were actually trying to tell me. Because it did feel like this book wanted me in there, reading and learning. It definitely was telling me something.

The directions said to be still, from deep inside. I could do that. Then I had to think about someone I loved. Okay, Abuelita came into my mind first. Next, I read that I should think of a difficult task that my loved one faced and imagine the task big, like an elephant. Then I should shrink the task elephant to a cow, and then to a dog. You get the picture. A few minutes later, I was imagining that task as a flea.

Yes, a flea! Who knows what a flea actually looks like? Not me. So I just thought small and bug-like. To be honest, I didn't even know what task I was working on. Did Abuelita have difficult tasks? She kind of made everything look easy.

So there I was, standing in the middle of her living room, thinking about fleas when I heard her calling me. It wasn't her usual call.

"Anastasia?" Then, after a very small (flea-like?) moment, "ANASTASIA!"

It was definitely a summons. I shot myself through the kitchen doorway, then stopped dead in my striped-legging tracks.

Minutes before, the kitchen counters had been covered in bowls of sauce and partially-chopped vegetables, grated cheese and tortillas, and chunks of beef. Pots had been bubbling and machines had been whirring. Noisy, messy, very controlled chaos.

Now, the table was set with candles and red-and-green napkins. Bowls of delicious-smelling food were crowded everywhere, and the rest of the kitchen was completely clean and tidier than I had ever seen it. Abuelita was out of her jeans; she was wearing a dress!

That tingle in my neck from earlier? It now felt like a herd of those fleas were dancing there.

"Sit down, Stazy," was all she said.

But her eyes had a whole lot more to say.

Hali

As if watching Evan and Clayton wasn't enough, I was also supposed to stir the soup Mom was making for dinner, and make sure it didn't burn. For once, Guy didn't seem to be around, so the boys were getting along pretty well.

I gave the soup a stir and pushed my brothers out into the backyard. Clayton wanted to play hide-and-seek, which didn't make sense to me at all because (a) how many places were there for three kids to hide in one small backyard and (b) Clayton had flaming red hair like mine, which made it so much easier to be found. Evan's hair was like Barnston's and Mom's, basic blah brown. But Clayton and I had Dad's hair and skin, that burned or freckled the minute someone even mentioned the sun.

But we hid and *seeked* about a hundred times. I hid in the tree and under the kiddy pool and behind the rose bushes. I found Evan under the barbecue and Clayton inside the garbage can.

I know! *Ewwwww*. He smelled too bad to play with after that, so I went back inside to check the soup. It was pretty good, but needed more salt. Mom never puts enough salt in her cooking, so I helped her out by adding a couple of spoons. Then I retested and it was so much better. Hopefully she'd agree.

From the window, I could see that Guy had shown up because both of my brothers were standing still, waving their arms excitedly as they looked in the same empty direction. No doubt explaining hide-and-seek etiquette to Guy.

Honestly. Who plays hide-and-seek with an invisible guy?

I tried to call Faye, but she didn't pick up. Probably in the garden again, or maybe at the animal shelter. Then I tried Rena, but there was no answer there, either. Probably reading that strange book about magic.

Of all the weird things that had happened since the new girl had shown up, Rena reading about magic was one of the weirdest.

What did any of us need to learn about magic?

Stazy

Abuelita and I . . . we're witches. You know, witches? Potions and spells and . . . hocus-pocus. That's us.

On that day six months ago, I read the words in that spell book and did my clumsy incantation and wham! Dinner was served.

It wasn't until later that I realized that Abuelita could have done the whole thing herself, of course, but she loved cooking the regular way, the fun and the mess and the surprises. And because she respected my dad's decision, she never used spells when any of us were around. Until she knew about me.

That day, as we ignored the food spread so beautifully on the table, she talked about a part of me that was a complete mystery. It was so weird, like two parts of me shaking hands for the first time.

She told me that her family had always been witches; that she'd been casting spells since she was a kid, like her parents and siblings. I didn't even have to ask if they were good spells or not. I knew what kind of person she was.

"What about Abuelo . . . was he a witch, too?" I asked.

"Oh yes, Anastasia. One of the best." She was watching me closely, waiting for the next question. "What about Dad?"

"We had four kids, your Abuelo and I, and three of them were witches. Your dad . . . no. For some unknown reason, it sometimes happens that the magic skips over certain people." I was listening harder than I ever had in my life. "So your dad has lived his life as a non-witch human. He married your mom; they had you and Ryan. Until today, that's the last we thought of it." She looked down at her plate of cooling food. "It didn't seem right, but we had to accept it. It felt like Ramon had been robbed of something so precious."

"But he was still your kid, same as the others, right?"

Abuelita grabbed both my cheeks and pinched them. "Of course! We are all the same, and all different. This was just a surprising way for us to be different from each other."

My mind was slowly whirring along, like an ink pen joining dots, with little blobs of ink spattering here and there. "So . . . how was Mom when he told her?"

Abuelita kept staring at her plate. When she finally looked up, I knew the answer, and I knew why her eyes were full of tears.

"He didn't tell her, did he? My mom doesn't know."

"No. He didn't. He lived his life completely outside of magic: his work, his hobbies, his friends. When he met your mom on the bus that day . . . "

Famous family story. Mom and Dad met on a bus, both of them with their noses in their books, not even noticing each other. Until Mom looked up and saw that he was reading the same book as her. He noticed her noticing him, took a look at her book—and the rest is history, I guess.

". . . they fell in love so fast, and then he was afraid to tell her, in case it made a difference. It was also sort of unimportant, he felt. He had never developed any magic, and was never going to. He was *not* a witch."

"And Ryan is not. And I am."

"Yes, my dearest. It seems that way." She looked so happy and so sad, all at the same time. Of course I knew why.

She leaned in and held out her arms, and we hung on to each other and to what had happened before and what was coming next.

"We need to tell my parents, don't we?"

"Yes." She stopped, as if she was desperately searching for an alternative. None.

"We do."

Faye

Mom reached over to give me a hug as I pushed on the door handle, halfway out of the car already. I leaned back in for her hug, then popped out the door, ready to go.

"I'll be back at five, ok?" she called.

"Yup. Bye, Mom!" I was off, down the winding path from the parking lot to the animal shelter.

I loved the animal shelter for so many reasons. One was that animals were my kinda people; I'd never met one I didn't like. Another reason was that the other volunteers and workers at the shelter were more like me than a lot of other people I knew. They felt calm and content around animals, and they knew that an animal's needs were just as important as a person's.

I also loved the shelter because even in the middle of our big city, it managed to look and feel like it was in the country. The path, the trees shading the pale-green building, and the large park area in the back felt like the best place for animals, and for me.

I could hardly wait to get inside and cuddle those critters. I couldn't sit still in school, but at the shelter I could ease a stray cat from its cage and sit quietly on the floor, murmuring and holding out my fingers until it realized the most sensible thing to do was jump right into my lap. Everybody at the shelter said the animals were comfortable with me faster than with anyone else. They were right. I did have an advantage they didn't know about, but it was still true.

Cuddling wasn't my only job, but my favourite one, definitely. I whipped off my jacket and said hi to Amy at the reception desk, then started the other jobs so I could get to the cuddling.

There was a pile of dirty feeding bowls in the back that needed washing. Then I cleaned all the cages that were empty and swept the floor.

Somewhere along the way, the people at the shelter had realized that plants were as happy with me as animals were, so I also did some gardening. This week there was a flat of winter pansies to be planted along the entry path. I'm not as good as Mom yet, but I'm learning.

I was in my Happy Place, all right. Hands in the dirt, surrounded by my favourite colour—green!—and looking forward to a massive cuddle fest in a short while.

My phone rang. My hands were so dirty that I stood up and wiggled my bum until the phone started to fall from my pocket. Mom would have given me the evil eye and Ginger would have rolled hers, but they weren't here, so they missed me catching it in the crook of my elbow. I balanced it there and saw that the call was from Hali.

For the first time ever, I didn't feel like answering. I was feeling so good, completely swallowed up in the things that fed me. Usually, we three were one of those things.

But lately, something didn't feel as safe there. It had started with the new girl, for sure, and the fact that she was in our Skills Class, in our space. But it was more than that.

Hali and Rena were having such different reactions to Stazy. Rena was trying to hide it, but I knew she wanted to be friends with her. Hali, being Hali, was all about loyalty to our group. She could sometimes be a little snooty, like about Stazy's clothes, but really, it wouldn't have mattered who Stazy was or how she dressed. Hali thought we were safest and happiest if we kept our group—and our secrets—to just us. It wasn't easy being different.

I let the phone keep ringing and eventually had to give in and use my dirty hands to get it back in my pocket. No amount of wiggling and elbow work was getting it back in there without fingers.

I finished up the pansies, washed my hands, and headed to the cages, still thinking. Three kittens from the same litter were in the first cage. One was ginger, one dark grey, and the last one a calico. They were grabbing at my hands before I could even unlock their cage, giving me baby nips and opening their tiny mouths wide and fierce. The sweetest little mews were all that came out. We were all rolling on the floor when Amy came in, but she was used to me. She laughed, grabbed the papers she needed, and disappeared again.

My body was rolling on the floor, but my head was still worrying about that problem. I was trying to figure out how I felt about Stazy, about being friendly or not, but all I could come up with was—confused. I liked to be friendly as much as the next kid, but I also knew what it was like to be teased for being different. It had taken Hali, Rena, and I a long time to become the strong, safe threesome we were. Was anything worth risking that?

I took a few dogs for walks, cooed at some animals that weren't well enough to come out of their cages, and cuddled all the cats I could find. I talked sensibly to a large boa constrictor in a glass case and less sensibly to a parrot who knew only five words.

Next thing I knew, Mom was texting my dirty phone from outside to let me know it was five o'clock. One more hand wash and I was out the door.

As usual, I left a lot of worries behind at the shelter. But this time, I couldn't quite get rid of that Stazy-worry.

I didn't phone Hali back that night because I had a pretty good idea what she wanted to talk about. I felt bad about it, but I avoided it.

I knew avoiding wasn't going to work much longer.

Rena

My phone was sitting there, looking at me.

Staring at me.

I ignored it, turning back to the magic book from the library. I wasn't really sure it should be called magic. It was more about being sneaky and deceptive, but all for fun. I loved it!

I was standing in front of the mirror, pretending to pull a pencil out of my nose and cram it into my ear. Ding dong dilly! After only thirty tries, it was really starting to look almost a bit believable. Almost.

I went back to the book to check out a new trick. I was feeling pretty awesome until I noticed the phone again. Just sitting there.

I REALLY wanted to call Stazy. Or, one-half of me did. The half that had a sore shoulder from hiding the pencil at a weird angle to pull off the last trick. The half that was having so much fun with this hokey magic book, and wanted to tell Stazy about it.

But the other half, the half that was closer to Faye and Hali than a cowgirl to her boots, was afraid to call in case it changed us three. I liked Stazy; I wanted to know her better. Maybe she'd be a perfect fourth for our group, even though we'd never needed a fourth. Maybe *she* needed to be a fourth.

Or maybe it would be a disaster.

It wasn't all about us. We had to think about what other people needed, too. Hali would say I was acting like an angel again, but that was okay, right?

So there was the phone. And I still didn't know what to do. I went back to the magic book and turned a page. One more magic trick, and then I'd decide.

This one involved poking a pencil through a full baggie of water. The chemicals in the baggie would hold the water in, the book said. I went into the kitchen and found a baggie and pencil. Harlan was in there too, doing something with chicken and a pan and a pile of spices that smelled really great.

I poured water in the baggie, then tried to poke the pencil through. No luck. The pencil was kind of dull, but I couldn't find the sharpener, so just kept poking at it.

"What in heaven are you doing, Rena?" Harlan abandoned his chicken for a minute to check out the baggie. "Aren't we going to end up with water all over the floor?"

Ahhh, the non-believer. The non-magical. I patiently explained the high level of magic I was involved in, and Harlan said he'd be happy to hold the bag for me, if that would help.

"I'm a magician! I have to perform these feats myself!" I huffed.

I poked. I poked again. I looked for the pencil sharpener. Nope. I poked and re-poked. Finally, I gave it a fierce, frustrated jab. The dull pencil tip tore at the bag and a fast dribble of water slid out, rapidly soaking my socks. Before we had a complete floor wash, I whipped it into the sink.

"Dang." That said it all.

"All the best magicians have assistants." Harlan was waltzing around the room, trailing his arms through the air as if he were demonstrating the finish of a wonderful trick.

"Okay, okay. You're hired."

He fished out another baggie while I continued my quiet hunt for the sharpener. I knew I'd been the last to use it, and didn't want to admit I hadn't put it back where it belonged. Harlan was a stickler for things being in the right place. He liked to comment that Alex and I were more the "place for everything and nothing in its place" kind of people.

"What are you looking for, Rena?"

"This!" I held up the sharpener, retrieved from the cereal cupboard. Victory. I sharpened madly, creating a deadly and precise pencil point.

I poured water in a fresh baggie, which my new assistant held as I prepared my weapon. His eyebrows were flying up and down as I calculated angles, whizzing the pencil back and forth in front of the baggie.

"Whoa. Be careful there, Mandrake."

I looked through the baggie at his watery face. "Mandrake?"

"Famous magician." He grinned. "Continue."

So I gripped the pencil tightly, pulled back once for force, and rammed it through the baggie.

There was a giant scream. My lovely assistant instantly dropped the baggie, which fell to the floor and soaked our feet. Harlan was leaping around, holding his hand and yelping in a very unprofessional way.

"Dad! Sorry! Oh gosh . . . let me see! Sorry!"

He stopped leaping long enough to hold his thumb up, which had a large piece of recently-sharpened lead sticking out of the fleshy part. I pulled at his hand, and he slowly let it down.

I gently pulled the pencil point out. Looking up at my dad with a little smile, I touched the bleeding spot. It looked purply and sore. I closed my eyes, and then ran my fingertips over it a couple times, like a 'kiss better' but with fingers.

When I opened my eyes again and looked down, my dad's thumb was whole and pink and happy again. He gave me one of his hugs, which I survived, and then said, "I'm going off shift for a while to finish this chicken, okay?"

"Sure, Dad. I'll practise that trick later." I wiped up the floor and started back to the living room. "On my own."

He nodded from the stove.

Then I was back in the living room with that phone. Before I could think any more, I picked it up and punched in the number I'd scribbled on a scrap of paper. Before I had time to rethink, a voice said, "Hello?"

"*Umm . . .* Stazy?"

"Yeah, it's Stazy. Who's this?"

My stomach was pounding. I could still hang up! But that would be so stunned.

"It's Rena. Serene, from school," I mumbled. "From Skills Class." My mouth just kept going. "You know, the coughing one?"

Double and triple drat and dang. This was ridiculous. What was I saying?

"Hi Rena. What's up?"

Be calm, be calm. "Not much. I was just calling because I remembered you practise magic, and I got this book from the library and . . . " I think I rambled on for about an hour, tripping over my words about the pencil-in-the-nose trick and the peril of Trick Number Two. There might have been a wooden laugh in there about damaging my assistant. Not sure.

Stazy said, "Really?" and, "That's great!" in a few spots. It was fine, and my stomach started to feel almost normal again.

"What are *you* doing?" I finally asked.

"Not much. I'm at my *abuelita's* place . . . that's my grandma. I'm just doing homework."

"Have you practised any magic today?" I had to ask. It was our interest in common!!

"Me? A little."

We said goodbye then. It wasn't much, but it made me feel happier than it did nervous.

Stazy was pretty quiet on the phone, but I had a feeling it made her feel the same way.

Stazy

I LOVED it that Rena called. Other than practising some magic with Abuelita, it was the best part of the day. Her call came right in the middle of me pretending to do homework. As usual, my brain had created two giant Ban Homework signs, one for each eyeball. Instead, that same brain was stuck on how my life had changed since that day six months ago.

There was no way to forget about Mom's reaction, her total flip-out when she found out Dad's family history and the fact that he'd lied about it. He said he didn't lie, he just didn't go into it, but Mom said that in this case that was the same as lying.

I heard a lot of stuff that they wouldn't have wanted me to hear, as our house just kind of blew up at that point. One night they were arguing when they thought I was asleep. Ryan was still out; he was out a lot after all this happened. Mom told Dad that she didn't think she'd ever be able to trust him again. She said that he'd passed something on to at least one of their kids that she had no idea about. It sounded like I had something terrible, like twelve eyeballs or green warts.

Come to think of it, I might end up with a few of those. Bad example.

I tried not to listen; but they were loud, and I was snoopy.

The thing was, they both sounded so, so sad, but my mom's anger was bigger than anything else. Nothing Dad said could change the huge fact that he hadn't told her something so important about his family, and now I was part of that family.

Luckily, it turned out that Ryan wasn't. He was so angry at the mess that magic had made of our family. When Abuelita did a couple of tests with him—he wasn't keen to do them, but he had to know—she found that he was like Dad. The magic wasn't there. Ryan was *sooo* glad. He picked his courses at university right after, and took almost all math courses. He told us he was going to be an accountant because that was as opposite to magic as he could get.

I felt completely different. Right from the start, I was good at magic. Like that first day, I could read the spell books easily, unlike every other kind of reading I'd ever done. It made Abuelita and I even closer than before.

But it made me different from Dad, even though he knew all about that life. And it made me very different from Mom and Ryan, who had no idea about that life, and didn't want to.

It was bad enough that Ryan was away at school, but knowing how mad he was made being separated worse. And knowing that he didn't accept such an important part of me was just something else that made me feel those first-day-of-school butterflies every day of the week.

The only thing that made it better was parkour. We'd shared that since he took me to my first class when I was six. He was already an awesome free runner by then. With Ryan training me and the classes I'd been taking, I'd become pretty good myself. It was hugely important to me, not only because it was fun and I was actually good at it, but because it held me and Ryan together on days when it seemed like magic was going to rip us apart.

"Anastasia? You haven't written anythin' down for five minutes. Are you stuck?"

Stuck? Of course I was stuck! It was school work.

"Maybe a little. Can you help me with this?" Abuelita made me slow down, she read me a few bits, and soon my page was finished. Not great, but finished.

"Now I need to talk to you about something, Anastasia." Fresh cups of tea, meringue cookies, and a very serious look on her face. I could feel my heart rummaging around in my toes. I'd had enough difficult discussions to last a whole lifetime. Another one?

"It's about your magic, and an initiation tradition that comes with it." She sipped her tea, left the cookies untouched. "I am bound to tell you about it because it is a long tradition in our culture. And you," she continued, tugging gently on one of my braids, "are now part of that culture." I could see in her face that for her, this was such a good-news/bad-news thing. Exactly the same as for me. Thrilled to be a witch, terrified at what it was doing to my family.

"Initiation like seven eyes of newt stirred in a bubbling cauldron at midnight in a haunted wood?" I was kidding, I think.

Abuelita laughed so hard that she spilled her tea. She waved her fingers at the spill, which dissolved as quickly as it'd appeared. She'd never done that before my magic appeared, but now it was a normal part of our existence. I was still working on it; if I'd tried that, there was an equal chance that the spill would wipe up beautifully, or that the whole tea pot would crack open.

"One too many witch movies for you, my girl." Abuelita wiped laughing tears from the corners of her eyes. "This initiation is what you might call a scavenger hunt, for items that will be important to you in your future."

Then she gave me a piece of school notebook paper with eight items listed in her messy scrawl. I squinted at the paper, trying to decipher her writing; my dyslexia was never an issue when magic was the subject. As always, Abuelita was giving me plenty of time to figure it out myself before she offered any help.

But all the tea spilling and homework avoiding must have taken longer than we thought because just then we both noticed the clock.

"I'm supposed to be home by five. Gotta hurry!" I didn't want to make Mom any more stressed than she already was.

I flew around the apartment grabbing my stuff, while Abuelita *magicked* food into containers for Mom and I to have for dinner. The last thing I crammed into my duffel bag was the list.

At the door, I gave Abuelita a giant hug. Then she loaded me down with the food bag. Even though it was kind of heavy, it wouldn't be cool if anyone saw the bag floating down the street, following me to the bus. Just before I left, she held my face between her hands and said, "The initiation is your choice. You need to ask your parents if they're okay with it. It's a hard choice, but I had to tell you."

The bag of food was making one shoulder droop. "Will I still have the magic if I don't do it?"

"You'll have some magic, but not enough. And you won't be a part of our witch culture, which is like a family." She was trying to stay neutral, I could see. But it wasn't working.

I knew neutral had nothing to do with it. Neither did asking my parents.

Hali

"*Pbbbffeeewt*!" Mom's cheeks were sucked in so far that she could have been a super model. "The soup!" We were all at the table for Sunday dinner.

I kept my head completely still and let my eyes wander from one face to the other around me. Barnston's face looked like Mom's, like he was breathing in before producing another blast on the tuba. The little boys hadn't touched their soup, of course. Dad looked completely happy, but of course, he was just like me. Couldn't get enough—

"SALT!" Mom was kind of rocking that super model glare-pout thing, as well as the sucked-in cheeks. She swiveled to face me. Even with *my* hearing, there was no pretending that I hadn't heard her. She was LOUD. I looked up from guzzling down my delicious concoction, my eyes as wide and surprised as I could make them. I could do a pretty good wide-eyed surprise.

"Hali. I asked you to stir the soup," she spluttered. "Not ruin it." Out of the corner of my eye, I could see Dad cramming spoon after spoon in; he knew what was coming. With his non-spooning hand, he reached back and pretended to scratch his ear, but I knew he was turning down his hearing aids, too. Guess he wanted to focus on all that salt before it was removed from the table.

"This is inedible. Destroyed. Ruined." I wasn't the only one pulling a little drama here. "Kaput." Dad kept slurping. "I wouldn't feed this to . . . " She looked up for inspiration, grasping for a suitable name. "I wouldn't feed this to Guy!"

Right away, Evan and Clayton started moaning. "Not fair!", and "Why pick on Guy?" But when she started reaching for our soup bowls to empty them into the compost, they both shut up. Any day they didn't have to eat soup was a good day, even if Guy had been slighted in the process. Dad and I didn't mind too much, as we'd managed to down most of the salty delight before Mom arranged its hasty removal from the table.

Confession time: I was guilty of being a drama princess from time to time, but my mom was a full-on drama queen about food. That's because she used to be a chef; in fact, that's how my parents met. Mom was doing her cooking thing on a private sailboat for some mega-rich people who adored really awesome food. Mom loved her job: the best ingredients at her fingertips, an appreciative foodie audience, sailing around the world on a gorgeous boat; what's not to love? Dad caught a glimpse of her one day as he was cruising past and was intrigued. I guess you could say the rest was history.

Or herstory. Or theirstory.

Mom still loved cooking, even though her days of caviar and *crème fraiche* were over, for now. We were more of a pizza and pasta crew, but everything Mom made tasted great.

Except for the salt thing. Salt was unhealthy, apparently, and any other spice was preferable. Well, I disagreed. Every dish needed a dash of salt. Well, maybe a sprinkle. Okay, let's say a scoop, or possibly a bucket.

Salt. *Mmmmm.*

Dinner was much less salty and pretty quiet after the soup disappeared. I excused myself as fast as I could and beat it to my room, where I closed and locked my door. Oh, that lovely lock. Can you spell "privacy"? My homework was done, so I went online for a while. You'll never guess what I found, even though I wasn't looking for it, of course. Of course.

Swimming! A swimming competition. I did a quick check that my door was really locked, then lost myself in those muscled bodies leaping off the pool edge, slicing through the water and folding themselves over to head back again. I could watch swimming for hours, which was not a great choice, according to my parents. So I hardly ever did.

But this time, I was already in big, salty trouble, so what was the harm of adding a little water to the mix? I eased back against my pillows, settled my eyes on that screen and lost myself in all that beautiful blue water.

Part 3
Two Friends, New Friends

Faye

Monday again. Goodbye animal shelter and gardening and leaning back against the cedars, feeling the love. Hello chained to a desk watching the clock hands snailing toward three o'clock.

Rena, Hali, and I were walking to school. Well, Hali was marching, Rena was kind of skipping, and I was pretty well snailing, like the clock hands. How we managed to keep in time was a mystery, but I guess that's what best friends are all about. Suddenly Rena halted in mid skip, sending all her fringes into a frenzy. She was staring into a bush by the sidewalk.

"Uh, Rena? I thought *I* was the Odd Behaviour Expert?" She was still staring at the bush. "No matter how hard you stare at it, that bush is not going to talk to you." Right then, of course, the bush let out a tiny, scared meowing noise.

Yikes! What was the matter with me? A kitten in distress, and I was too tensed up about Monday to have my sensors out?

Hali was still marching down the sidewalk, eager to blast into another week of using extreme academic brilliance to prove that a hearing loss was no biggie. She finally realized that she'd lost Rena and me, and halted her military attack. "C'mon, you two. Tardy is no way to start the week!"

Tardy? Who says "tardy"? Every weird thing Hali said, though, sounded like a word trend waiting to happen.

"There's a kitten here, Hali. A sweet little kitty." Rena almost purred herself. She was edging closer, but the kitten slowly moved away from her, still mostly hidden under the bush. I moved to the other side of the bush and held my hand out.

"Kit-ty!" Rena whispered. She oozed comfort and sweetness and light. Rena was the real thing; she really was all those things. But the kitten moved away.

"Kitty?" she tried again, not so sure now.

I leaned down and put out my hand and waited. Hali and Rena watched as the kitten sniffed the air once, then sidled right up to my outstretched fingers.

"Kitty!" Rena said, not so purr-y now. Then she added, "I think that might be the new girl's cat. Remember her six words were about her kitten?" She was scrunching up her forehead very dramatically and squeezing her eyes almost shut. It looked to me like she was either having a gas pain or was trying to pretend she was remembering something. I picked the second one.

"I think the kitten's name is Carter."

"So this is Stazy's house, Rena? You know that?" Hali's voice was a bit principal-ish.

"I'm pretty sure." Her eyes and forehead had gone back to normal, now that the remembering or the gas were done.

But maybe not. Now her eyes were bugged out wide, like a comic book exaggeration of someone getting a bright idea. All that was missing was the light bulb over her head.

"How about if I take Carter up to the door?" she said. Not much of an idea for that light bulb look. What was she up to? So un-Rena-like!

"Really, Rena? And risk an allergy attack?" Hali sounded a little grumpy about the whole situation, but I know she was just watching out for Rena. I'm sure the tardy possibility was bothering her, too.

"I'll do it," I said. I reached forward and scooped the adorable little furball into my hand. The purring started immediately. My instincts told me that Carter was a male, and they also told me he was way too young to be roaming around outside by himself. So I borrowed Hali's march, right up Stazy's sidewalk to her front door.

When she answered my knock, her eyes bugged out like Rena's had, only on her, it looked authentic.

"Carter! How did you get out?" Her hands reached out and grabbed the kitten in a flash. Then she registered me, and a second later, Rena and Hali at the end of the sidewalk. "Thanks, Faye." Maybe I was frowning, because she kept going. "He's never gotten out before. I'm really careful." She must have been feeling guilty, 'cuz she leaned around me and said it again in a louder voice, so Hali and Rena would hear.

"No problem. Bye, Carter." I wiggled my nose right up near his, and he pushed his soft paw along my cheek.

"Wow," Stazy said. "Never seen him do that before." She took Carter down a hall and disappeared into a doorway.

What can I say? To animals, I'm a rock star. Not so much to teachers, which made me think of school and the tardy issue.

"Let's go, Faye!" Hali was really impatient now. So we whistled down Stazy's walk and we all did Hali's march as we turned in the direction of the school. We probably should have waited for Stazy. I mean, she would be out the door in a second. It would have been the nice thing to do; Rena kept peeking behind us, 'cuz she's a little nicer than Hali and me.

But for some reason, we didn't.

Stazy

I thought they might still be there when I came out, but I thought wrong. They were long gone. I carefully locked the door and dropped my key into my backpack, right beside Abuelita's list. I still wasn't sure about doing it, partly because I couldn't understand what even one single item was. But it didn't feel safe leaving it at home, either.

As I hurried toward the school, my mind wandered back to the days before my witchiness was unveiled. I never thought about 'safe', in those days. My family was safe, my home was safe, my life was safe. Was magic worth all that? I felt angry; so what else was new? But only a few steps farther, I knew the answer to my question.

I wanted it all—safety and magic. Why not? I figured I deserved them both.

I was late for school, so my second week of school started pretty much the same as my first. In front of the class, all eyes on me. It was becoming a familiar pattern.

But at least I had my answer now.

The list was on.

Hali

All day long, in our regular class and even in Skills Class under Mr. Locke's very watchful eyes, Stazy kept pulling out this piece of paper from her backpack. Believe me, I was *not* watching her, but it was impossible not to notice. Pull the paper out, read the paper, look up at the ceiling, frown, put the paper back. Repeat. Repeat. Repeat.

I knew that she had trouble reading; we were obviously all in Skills Class for a reason, and it hadn't been hard to figure out that hers had to do with reading and writing. Was she really just trying to read what was on that paper every time she looked at it? Stripy legs and all, she wasn't my favourite person, but I could feel her pain on the comprehension issue. I could read and write extremely well, but comprehending the spoken word? Very tricky, very often. Another of Mr. Locke's words came to mind. I didn't much like her, but I could *empathize* with Stazy. A bit.

Monday lunch was the first day for a bunch of the school clubs to begin. Faye was at a Garden Club meeting, Rena was no doubt making her fringes frizzle at choir practice, and I was at the first cross-country meeting. I was a natural fit, but it always bummed me out a little that I couldn't join the Debate Club, which I would also have been stellar at. I could argue the mane off a lion. But if I didn't clearly hear the rebuttals, how useful was I to the team? You could only say "Pardon me?" so many times before serious eye rolling would begin.

Naturally, our meeting was outside and involved a little run around the school perimeter. I was jogging along, getting into my happy zone, when those eye-bruising striped tights accosted my vision, yet again. I guess there was no Magic Club or Kitten Club or Weird Costumes Club, because Stazy was outside the schoolyard, on the sidewalk of a house across the street. So weird. What was she doing on their sidewalk? For that matter, what was she doing outside the schoolyard? That was a no-no right there.

But I didn't have time to worry about it because I was at the front of the pack of joggers, and I intended to stay there. When I burst by for a second time, she was off the sidewalk and on their lawn, looking up at a big tree. I confess, this was getting so odd that it pushed me to run even faster, just to get around the yard in time to catch the next instalment of Stazy Striped Legs' Strange Adventure.

Gadzooks. (I learned that word all by myself, and had thought more than once about teaching it to Mr. Locke as payback for all the good ones he'd taught me.)

The next time around, she was up on a branch of the tree, reaching *way* out toward something. I almost shrieked, but keeping ahead of the pack was using up most of my air and I wanted to stay there. As I stared and ran, she swung her legs for momentum and lunged for something. I think she got it, whatever it was. Then she did a flip in midair and landed as light as a cat on her feet. So weird!

The last time past, she had somehow completely disappeared. Talk about magic! I had a good look at the tree, though, and I think it was an apple tree. So Stazy was swiping an apple from somebody's yard.

Luckily, I could run *and* think at the same time. Had she forgotten her lunch? Was she so hungry that she'd been driven to theft? Where did she learn to climb and flip like that? She sure didn't look the type. Was she hiding somewhere now, eating her criminal gains?

Or, maybe not. Maybe it was a special apple, something she'd tuck in that backpack she'd been fiddling with all morning. Maybe she'd spend the afternoon alternating between peeks at the paper and peeks at the apple. That little bit of *empathy* I'd felt earlier in the day disappeared. I could hardly wait for the walk home, to catch Faye and Rena up with all this papering and apple-ing.

So weird.

Stazy

I'd been sneaking subtle peeks at school, but it was a few days later before I felt really comfortable pulling out the list and the apple and looking at them at home. Up until then, Mom was so tired when she got home from work that she collapsed on the couch, dozing off until she decided it wasn't too embarrassingly early to actually go to bed. Tonight was different, though. She'd taken the laptop into her room with serious writing intentions. When I peeked in her doorway, her head was down and her fingers were moving. I was glad for her because writing for her was like magic for me—necessary!

I was also glad because it meant I could have a serious look at Abuelita's list. I guess I could have looked at it in the privacy of my own room. But really, my room was so small that I might not have been able to unfold the paper all the way. Tiny exaggeration there, I guess, but not much. My room consisted of my bed, a dresser and a closet. If the dresser drawers weren't pushed all the way back in, the closet door wouldn't open. I hated it, especially when I remembered my old bedroom in the house we should still be living in. I could have left all the dresser drawers out, and both my closets would still open. And that was more my style. This enforced neatness was horrible.

So I was in the living room. The one advantage of this little old house was that it had a real fireplace. I guess newer homes had gas fireplaces, like our old house. But this one had real fire, with real logs. Mom had done some groaning about the mess and the clean-up, but when I'd promised to help with that, she'd relented and got some firewood. Tonight, before she vamoosed into her room to write, she'd shown me how to lay the fire and had started it for me. There was a large side order of warnings never to do it by myself, and she stared at me very hard as she said this. Both of us knew how much I loved fire. Flames. Even gas flames, but this was totally better.

It was kind of a weird thing, that warning. Because I'd loved fire from before I could remember. As a baby, my parents had to watch me like hawks around campfires or candles. That had always just been a

Stazy thing. But now, it felt to me like my mom's warning and staring were because it was something else. It was a witch thing.

So part of me settled in by that fire, feeling a purr inside that rivalled Carter's, who was curled up beside me. Another part was angry, as usual. Why did I have to have a label, be a witch or a non-witch? Why should I have to fall into someone else's categories? I didn't create this problem, and I didn't want to have to choose. I just wanted to be me. Stazy.

Rena

The phone was tempting me again. I really wanted to call Stazy.

In our group or out of our group. Who really cared? I was tired of all the hogwash. Striped leggings. Again, who really cared?

She was an interesting kid and so were we. Who needed the labels?

Faye

It was still bugging me that we hadn't waited for Stazy that day. I felt a little bit like a mean girl in one of those hyped-up movies, and I didn't like the feeling.

We were keeping her out, putting a big "Not One of Us" label on her forehead.

Mean.

Hali

Even shutting off my hearing aids couldn't completely obliterate Barnston's tuba. But even Barnston's tuba couldn't completely obliterate the memory of Stazy, standing in that yard all alone. Staring at a tree, of all things.

Strange, but also sort of sad. Maybe she wasn't just one thing, but a mix of things.

But was it worth it to find out?

Stazy

I finally unfolded the paper and pressed it flat with my somewhat-sweaty hand. I'd pulled it out a million times at school, but this was the first time I'd really read the whole thing. Abuelita's words jumped out at me, messy but dyslexia-free. Everything about doing magic seemed easy for me. It was just *being* magical that was so hard.

The paper was labelled "Anastasia's Initiation List". That part was easy. But the list itself?

1. Two locks from whence you came
2. Music from the ocean, made for a tale
3. A sweet nibble
4. The key to nature
5. Fire and her friends
6. Two halves made whole
7. You and Ryan, not runnin'
8. Adam's apple wings

The fourth time through, I picked up my phone and texted Abuelita. Luckily, she answered right away.

Abuelita, this list doesn't make any sense!

You don't think so, querida?

I thought it would be like finding four pinecones and a used dog leash . . . that kind of thing.

It's not that kind of a scavenger hunt, Anastasia. Why would I create something like that for you?

But these are all mysteries! I don't have a clue what I'm looking for. And then immediately after, *Wait! YOU made this up???*

Of course I did. Who else? It's an initiation challenge from the person inside the culture who knows you best. That's me. And I know it's a little hard, right? It's challenging for a reason.

No kidding. (I added a pouty emoji after that.)

Easy would mean nothing. How badly do you want to join this culture?

There was a pause in the texts while I thought about that one. Then I leapt back in.

How will I even know the objects when I see them? I KNOW what a pinecone looks like, but . . . a key to nature? Fire and her friends? C'mon.

You'll know, Anastasia. There was another pause here, but I could see by the moving dots on my screen that Abuelita was typing more.

Even if you don't know right away, you will eventually.

I groaned so loud that I woke Carter from his snooze. But there was more.

No magic on these, right, querida? This is your initiation into the culture, so you can't use the culture to get there.

For now, I was all out of words, so I sent a thumbs-up, a heart, and clicked off my phone.

Rena

The more I tried to think less about the phone, the less I thought less and the more I thought more. See? I was dang confused.

By Thursday, I was spending more time avoiding whispers from a piece of metal and plastic than talking to real people, so I finally just picked up my phone and punched in Stazy's number.

"Hello?"

My head was so stuffed with ways that this conversation was going to be different than the first—no rambling, no blabbing about things I'd had no intention of talking about—that I could only get one doggone word out.

"Stazy?" Yes, Stazy. It was *her* phone.

"Yes?" And a pause. A long pause. Well, I sure wasn't rambling. Finally, I just let 'er rip.

"Hi, Stazy. Yeah, it's me. It's Rena. Hi. How are you doing? How's Carter? I'm sure glad we found him that day. Actually, I found him, but he wouldn't come to me. I think he was super scared. But Faye's amazing with animals. She was the one who got him out of the bush.

What are you doing right now? Have you finished the homework? I'm almost done the homework." Luckily, my breath gave out there so I had to pause. While I grabbed another lungful of ammunition, Stazy got a few words in.

"Fine. Yeah, thanks. Not much."

I had beaten around the bush so much that it had no leaves left on it, so I got right to the point. "Do you want to hang out sometime?"

"Sure, Rena. Yeah, I would."

"How about, like, maybe tomorrow?" I was trying to think fast, keep ahead of my out-of-control mouth. "How about the candy store by the library after school? Maybe four?"

"Yup. I know where that is."

"Okay."

"Okay."

"Okay! See you then, Stazy."

"Bye, Rena."

Done! Finished! I stuck my tongue out at my phone and tossed it on my bed, and felt really great for about two seconds. Then I thought about Faye and Hali, and how I'd made my meet-up time with Stazy for four, after I'd walked home with them and could go back out again without them knowing about it.

Unbelievable. My phone had started with the whispering again—a lot of things around me seemed to have supernatural powers lately!—but this time it wanted me to call two people.

And I couldn't.

Stazy

Thursday! What a day! Parkour! Dad! And maybe I even had a friend. It was almost enough to balance out that list and the apple that was rotting in my school bag. I didn't know why I'd decided that one of the apples off that tree by the school might be number eight on the list, Adam's apple wings. Really, it was just an apple, now a rotting apple. But maybe someone in that house was named Adam? Any which way I looked at the apple, it didn't have wings. But still, I didn't throw it away. I thought I'd just run it by Abuelita with the seven other things that I knew I would find soon. Ha!

I was wearing my parkour outfit of black shorts and neon-green t-shirt. I know. Neon green. So un-black. But I'd gotten used to it, having taken parkour for six years. I waited by the window in the living room, knowing that Dad wouldn't want to come to the door. The polite, stiff conversations I'd heard between my parents after the shouting had stopped were horrible to hear, and I knew I'd rather leap out the door when the car appeared than have to listen to another one.

"Bye, Mom!" I called when Dad's Volvo pulled up. "See you after dinner!" Thursday it was parkour first, dinner with Dad second. All the details of the kid-sharing thing weren't totally sorted out, but Thursdays were sacred.

"Hi Dad!"

"Stazy." He was waiting for me beside the car, and I jumped up into his arms. I was so glad to see him, but so sad that it was just here and there. Too bad I hadn't known my whole stupid life how great it was to have both parents with me all the time. Too late, now.

His voice sounded like I felt. When he finally put me down, he said, "How's my girl?" And he looked at me carefully, searching for trouble.

"Okay, Dad." I smiled at him, he smiled at me and then we climbed into the car. It wasn't everything, but it was better than nothing.

When I sat down, the neon on my t-shirt bulged out at the stomach, meeting up with thighs that seemed to spread quite a way over the seat. My eyes saw it, but I didn't care. I was with Dad and I was heading to parkour, where I was the best in my class. My body gave me strength.

We caught up the best we could on the drive, and then it was into the gym. It was filled with rails for vaulting, bars for swinging, and walls for climbing. There were mats, foam pits, and obstructions everywhere; things that would have me jumping and landing and running in no time.

As we warmed up, I glanced over to the parents' seating to find Dad, just to be sure. Yup, he was there. After that, it was an hour and a half of pushing myself, flying around the gym until my sweat had that neon-green shirt stuck to my back like a turtle in mud. As always, I had the best time. Until magic had come along, parkour was the only place I did things right; it was the very opposite of standing in front of the whiteboard at school with no idea what everyone else saw written there.

At dinner, Dad and I talked and talked and talked. We didn't go near witchcraft, even though that was what had caused all the problems; witchcraft was my Dad's family, not my Dad. But we went over everything else. It was easier with Dad than Mom because we were on the same page. He just wanted to come home, and that's what I wanted, too.

But at the end of the night after another big hug, he dropped me off and stayed glued to the curb until I was inside, the door was locked, the porch light was off. Night, Dad.

Hali

I *loved* weekends. Not because I could sleep in and shut off my brain and eat junk food. No way! I had things to do. I could get up early, go for runs, spend extra time on my homework, improve my vocabulary, hang out with my besties and . . . READ.

I could lose myself in a book so fast that it would make your ears ring. (Well, if you had ears that could hear much). I loved non-fiction because I could learn about Greek beaches and starfish and sailboarding. I loved novels even more because I could hop right into someone else's life and roam around with them until Barnston's tuba or a calamity with the little boys dragged me back.

Calamity. What a word. It even sounded like trouble. Thank you,

Mr. Locke!

So there I was, Friday night in my dreamy beachy bedroom with a brand new spine-never-cracked novel, a giant glass of water, and my favourite snack, seaweed. And really, with a set-up this perfect, I was going to do all I could to protect it. So against orders, I pulled out both hearing aids and felt the welcome rush of silence. Settling back against the pillows, I pulled my knees in close and balanced my book there.

Chapter One. Girl works at her parents' beachside restaurant.

Hmmm . . . I stopped reading to think about that. That's how I read. Read a bit, think a bit, daydream a bit. Repeat. What would it be like, working for your parents? At least you'd know you'd have a job. But imagine them bossing you around at home all day and then at work, too. A job would be good, though. I knew I'd save all my money for things I wanted that no one else around there wanted. Like a beach holiday!!

Okay, back to the book. Chapter Two. Her best friend was a boy. That had always been okay, but now that they were older, it was somehow getting awkward.

Hmmm . . . I'd never had really close friends until Rena and Faye. Before that, my hearing issue hadn't been diagnosed, and that made things hard. I just couldn't figure out what was going on around me as a little kid, and wondered how all the other kids magically knew when it was time to share the playdough or get out of the wading pool. Hearing aids made my life so much better. Better, but not perfect.

A boy for a best friend? I couldn't imagine. I guess maybe if he liked running and reading and the ocean, knew a lot of words, was focused and organized, hated tubas . . .

I was about to lunge into Chapter Three when my own best friends lurched back into my daydream. I was suddenly remembering our walk home after school that day, same route as always. Fridays we always turtled along. No tardy worries, right? The weekend stretched invitingly before us, and we had the whole day at school to discuss, plus our weekend plans, some together, some apart.

But today, Rena, who could amble with the best of them, had nipped along the sidewalk as if Beyoncé was waiting at her place to do a duet. When Faye asked her to slow down, she looked stricken and slowed to a crawl for about a minute, then started off at a pace that frizzled her fringes all over again.

"What's up with the need for speed, Rena?" I asked.

"Me? S-s-speed?" she stammered.

Then she slowed right down and kept herself there, but I saw her sneak a couple peeks at her phone, checking the time. Something had definitely been up with that girl.

It was almost like she had been keeping something from us, which was a completely weird feeling for me. It had never happened before. I could trust Faye and Rena with any secret, and of course, I did. We trusted each other with secrets it wouldn't have been safe for anyone else to know.

But today had felt different. What was Rena up to? The only thing I could figure out was that with Faye's birthday coming up, she had some secret shopping to do. She hadn't wanted to say it in front of Faye, of course, but she'd be blabbing to me before the weekend was out. That was it. For sure.

I dove back in to Chapter Four, sure I had everything figured out, as usual.

Rena

It was perfect. Well, almost perfect. It was jelly beans and grins that after a while, became laughing. We talked about school and music and food and allergies and Mr. Locke.

Most of it was fun talk, but a little bit was even serious. I told Stazy all about my dads, and at first, she didn't say much about her family. When she finally did, she told me a little about her mom. Full stop. Then a little about her dad. Another stop. Then her brother Ryan, away at university. Again with the stop.

"So, your mom and dad aren't together?"

Her eyes behind those black-framed glasses were huge. She shook her head and start telling me about her grandma, except she used the Spanish word, *abuelita*. There was no holding back when Stazy talked about her grandma. No siree Bob! Stazy got so excited and bubbly—I know, it surprised me, too!—and blurted out stuff about her grandma's funky apartment and cool style and great cooking and fierce Stazy-love.

Then she started on other people in her family. She told me that she looked like one of her cousins, but had the temperament (Wow! Mr. Locke word!) of an uncle.

When she asked about my grandmas, I told her about mine, and even a little bit about my grandpas, cousins, aunts and uncles. Lots to talk about. But my mind was a little slowed down, back thinking about her looking and acting like other people in her family.

I'd never have that. My family was so great, and I was glad they were mine. But being adopted, I'd never catch myself in the mirror looking like cousin Laila, or hear myself saying something that sounded just like Uncle Pete. I guess that was okay. But still. What would that be like?

Anyway, we made a plan to meet again, which made my heart sing. My head was littering the song with words like "Faye", "Hali" and "fess up!", but my heart was still singing.

For some reason, something powerful was drawing me to Stazy. She just seemed so . . . right. I couldn't explain it any more than that, and that was just too feeble to even try opening my mouth about to Hali or Faye. So my mouth stayed shut.

Hali

No word, not one, about Faye's birthday from Rena. No whispered plans to buy a cowboy hat with animals on the brim. No sketches falling from her backpack of gluten-free cakes topped with flowers and the animal shelter.

Was she trying to surprise me, too? If so, she was succeeding. I was starting to feel inordinately surprised. Right, Mr. Locke?

Faye

I would scour the gym shower stalls to avoid class time. I would interview all of Mom's patients about their sock-changing habits to avoid class time. I would trim the nose hairs of our custodian to avoid class time.

Ew, no. Not that last one. Even *I* have limits.

But a middle-of-the-day pep rally, fourth week of school, to cheer on our track team? A no-brainer, even with the humungous noise factor! I was kind of a quiet water trickling and rabbits sniffing and flowers waving fan, but I could bear the noise for a short while. Especially since Hali was one of the stars of our school track team.

By the time I got to the gym, it was almost full. I scanned the crowd for Rena, who of course had saved me a seat. How did she know I'd be late? Mystery.

The room was jumping. There were kids crammed onto the bleachers with the odd adult thrown in for crowd control. Kids were piled on stairs and along the bannisters, and of course, some were hanging out near the doors, ready to attempt a quick getaway once the teachers were busy getting the rest of us pepped up.

Before the team was introduced, I looked to my left and saw Mr. Locke and Stazy—sitting together! He waved, and pointed at a couple of spaces still vacant by them. (Who wants to sit by a teacher, even a great one like Mr. Locke, right?) I think my grin back was all tooth and no heart, but I mumbled to Rena that we'd better go down there. She didn't seem bothered one bit. When we got there, she plunked herself right beside Stazy, so I took her other side.

It was okay. At least I wasn't sitting right beside a teacher. But I found myself hoping that Hali was too busy running around and waving at the crowd to notice us all together.

Hali

Runners? Check. Black and white, serious yet stylish. Outfit? Check. School colours, inevitably, red and yellow, so not *my* colours. But considering the things I couldn't change, I still looked pretty good!

Hair? Check. In a high ponytail, hanging dramatically down my back, perfect for bobbing up and down as we did laps around the gym.

Hearing aids? Check. The noise would be deafening (not a problem for me!), but I needed my aids in top form in case there were any surprises, like calling out my name or asking me to say a few words. The dork factor of waving at the wrong time or not walking up to the microphone when called had haunted my dreams the night before.

Then, the team was announced and we jogged lightly to the centre of the gym.

Yup. Deafening!

Rena

Life was getting so complicated. There I was, sitting between Stazy, my new friend, and Faye, one of my two best friends. Everybody was so pumped! Kids were cheering, kids who spent most of their day being so cool that it was hard to tell if they were breathing, sometimes. For once, everyone in the gym was acting as crazy as me! It was complete heaven. Doggone!

Except that I had to pretend that I wasn't thrilled that Mr. Locke had called us down. Except that I was trying to make the Stazy side of my face look thrilled and the Faye side of my face look bummed. It felt like some kind of facial exercise to prevent wrinkles, but I think I was getting them anyway, just thinking about it all.

And then there was the matter of Hali. Luckily, she was just too busy with the yelling and waving to have any time to look for us in the—

Hali

—bleachers! One look up and there they were, the Four Musketeers. Mr. Locke, Stazy, Rena, and Faye.

I kept jogging, but I'm pretty sure my ponytail lost about half its bob. Leave them alone for half an hour, and they were hanging out with teachers and that stripy-legged girl.

I had a brief flash of Stazy standing beneath that apple tree, alone, but I pushed it right out of my mind and picked up my pace, passing two of my teammates and throwing our carefully-measured pace way off kilter. The kids in the bleachers started cheering even louder, which suited me just fine.

Stazy

Homework. Again. After hours in classrooms, hunched over books with little worms of print meandering this way and that, I was supposed to come home and take up worm-watching again.

The only good thing about watching the print wriggle was that it reminded me of snakes. I liked 'em. I liked how they slithered up slow and easy, eyes wide open to take everything in. I liked how they loved eating meat. Yum. And I liked that most people didn't like them. I'd love a pet that made people a little nervous; if I was going to feel left out, I might as well be *really* left out.

Don't get me wrong. I adored Carter, and I knew that my chances of having a snake for a pet were zilch. The combination of finding out I was a witch and then me asking for a pet snake would send Mom right over the edge, so that was out. But still. *Hisssss.* Maybe some day.

Then I thought about Rena, and my heart lifted up a little. I wasn't quite as left out as I had been when school started. And I doubted Rena would like snakes much.

Back to the homework. *Bleh.*

Bzzt! Bzzt! Yay—a text! Homework, be still!

Hey, Staz! How's stuff? It was Ryan!

Ok. U?

Yup, good. You getting to the gym?

Just Thursdays, with Dad. Long way from our new place. Still getting used to school, and bussing.

Right. Keep at it, sis. You're good.

I miss running with you, Ryan.

Me too. Have you nailed that flip I demo'd?

Not yet. Still working on it.

Ok. Gotta go.

Coming home soon?

Dunno. Miss you, Staz.

Me 2.

Was he texting Mom and Dad? I doubted it. And he didn't even ask about them.

I looked over the messages again, and my heart dropped down a little from its Rena lift. The messages were really all about parkour. Did he ever talk to me about anything else? And now that he was far away at school and he didn't seem to want to have anything to do with our family, would we just end up talking about flips and jumps?

Didn't sound like much of a relationship, really.

Homework. Again.

Rena

It was one of those days when it seemed like Autumn was campaigning to win Most Beautiful Season. "Look at me! Look at me! Flame and mustard and pumpkin-orange, all brighter and deeper than Winter or Spring or even that show-off, Summer!"

Today, I had to agree. It was a day to take your breath away. Even if your breath was a bit wheezy because there was something weird (but colourful!) in the air that made your nose itch and your lungs wobble.

Stazy and I were meeting again; the third time! I'd decided to avoid the candy store this time. Maybe a moving target was harder to spot? Anyway, there was no track practice and Faye would never willingly go near the school unless she had to, so I knew no one would see us there.

"Okay, how about across the street from there, by that old apple tree?" Stazy had said.

I was so glad she didn't ask why we were switching from the candy store that I said "Yup!" immediately. It wasn't till later that I wondered how she knew where that apple tree was. She'd been at school for a month, and I hadn't noticed it after mega years of being there.

I was early, so I sat under the tree, angled away from the window of the house. It was kind of weird to meet in someone's yard, so I was glad to be hidden. But the tree *was* awesome, stripes of yellow and red and orange running through its leaves. I thought about Stazy's orange-and-black tights, and wondered if that was the appeal?

Then I remembered something she'd said last time, at the candy store. We were eyeing up all the jars of old-timey candy, figuring out what to get. Stazy took forever, looking carefully at the names on every single jar.

"You looking for a certain candy, Stazy?" I'd asked.

She looked at me hard for a second, like she was deciding if she should say something. Then she said, "I thought I remembered a kind of candy called 'Adam's apple wings'. Maybe they have it here?"

So we both checked. We even asked the store clerk, a teenager who wasn't that interested and just wanted to get back to her studying. No luck. In the end, I bought anything without my allergens in it, and Stazy got a bunch of fizzy candy that made little explosions in her mouth.

But even as we left, she was still checking those jars one last time, looking for Adam's apple wings. Something had really been bugging her, I could tell. The fizzy candies were all fine, but she was lookin' like she'd just had a bath in a barbed-wire bathtub.

So as I sat under that tree waiting, I thought about those Adam's apple wings again. Maybe this tree wasn't about orange stripes, after all. I got up, still staying out of sight from the gosh-darn house.

I started to look carefully into the leaves, wondering what an Adam's apple wing could look like. I was really concentrating hard. I forgot all about the house and the school across the street and, I guess, a couple of other important things, too.

Part 4

Surprises

Stazy

Slamming the door behind me, heading for the school. My head felt buzzy, so I gave it a little shake. Waved at Carter, sunning in the window, then turned toward the school.

"Thinking too much about that list," I mumbled. And it was true. Trudged one block, two, three. It seemed like in every alone moment, I had the items from that dratted list popping and fizzing in my brain, like a fireworks display that just wouldn't end.

A sweet nibble . . . *BAM! BAM!* I was nearing the school now, so crossed the street toward the yard with the tree in it.

Two halves, made whole. . . *BAM!* I could almost see the tree now.

And the one that was bugging me the most, for some reason—Adam's apple wings. *BOOM!*

The tree was clear now. Rena was there.

She was looking up into the leafy mess of reds and oranges. The shock of whitey-blonde hair falling down her back caught my eye first, but something was weird. Her head seemed too close to the leaves. She was so high up . . .

Then I looked at her feet.

She was hovering off the ground. Hanging in the air. I closed my eyes for a second, shook my head, then looked again.

Flying. Rena was flying.

KABOOOMMM!!

Rena

Behind me, I heard a little noise. Like a gasp. My brain clicked on, and my heart clutched. And then I was on the ground in a heap. The wheezing started one second later.

I could feel my breaths getting shorter and shorter. It felt like all my organs were seizing up. I could feel myself being pulled up, could feel Stazy shoving her shoulder under my arm and run-walking me down the street. The little bit of my brain still there was trying to stay calm, keep breathing, move my legs to help Stazy.

I don't know how long it took to get to my door, or who answered. I don't know how I got to my bed, or which medicine they gave me. I only remember Stazy backing slowly from the door after she'd delivered me home. Her eyes behind those glasses were huge, boring right into the real Rena.

She'd seen. Stazy had seen me fly.

Breathe. Breathe. Breathe.

Stazy

Suddenly the Adam's apple wings seemed a little less important.

Magic tricks? Really strong legs? What on *earth* had I just seen?

Or was it from earth at all?

Faye

Finally October. That meant I could flip the calendar on September. One month of school down, nine to go. Talk about good news, bad news.

First period, Skills Class. Stazy was away, so it was just Hali, Rena, and me, like the old days. I kept peeking at Rena, who looked absolutely green. My favourite colour—trees, grass, frogs! But not so much on people. She told us she'd had an allergy attack the day before, something about an apple tree. She looked awful.

Mr. Locke was starting up with the vocabulary words again, so Hali was in heaven. She had her notebook out, and was printing today's word, *stupefaction*. I glanced at her book, where her word was printed. It looked like a calligrapher had dropped by and painted the word onto her page. I looked at mine. It looked like a second grader's first time doodling with a pen. We were supposed to be finding other words that meant the same: you know, cinnamons. No. Synonyms.

Hali would write, then stop and look up into the air, then look

78

down at her page and write something. Look up, find another word, look down, write. I couldn't think of any, so I looked up there, just to see if there were words printed on the ceiling that I hadn't heard about. But no. If they were printed up there, it was something only Hali could decipher. Of course. My bee was back, so I spent a little time watching it circle lazily over my head. It hadn't been around for a while, so it was kind of fun, watching its little yellow-and-black fuzziness explore the air.

Ahhemmm. One of those quiet throat noises that Mr. Locke makes to bring me back to earth. I nodded my head at him, then let it drop over my book. I wrote *surprise.*

I noticed that Rena wasn't writing much, either. She was pulling a Faye: staring out the window, with an unusual little frown line rumpling her forehead. Rena was not a worrying person, so that gave me something else to think about. Something else besides stupefaction. Hali just kept on writing.

"I need to step out for a minute, kids. I'll be right back," Mr. Locke said. *Yaay!* Full on daydreaming time for Faye!

He left, and Rena and I put our pens down. I was ready to zone out, but Rena looked like she was ready for something else.

"Hali? Faye?" she began.

Stazy

Questions, questions.

How did Carter manage to get out the door without me seeing? I was probably half asleep, after the night I'd had. Since when did kids get insomnia? Maybe since they saw friends floating up in trees? And when my eyes finally did close, it was dreams about flying lists and apple trees with heads for branches. Very restful.

I knew my reaction was weird, because there I was with my *own* secret that would blow the fringed boots off Rena. But I just couldn't figure it out. She'd told me she was practising magic tricks, but was there really a magic trick to fly you up into a tree, no props in sight?

So now I was late, what with getting Carter back in the house. It was kind of nice though, walking to school with no other kids on the street. Forget walking! I'd run the whole way, even hopping up and down curbs and jumping onto a couple stone fences along the way.

Although I was whipped when I got to school, my head felt clearer than it had since the day before. But as I checked in at the office and headed to Skills Class, the strange feelings ramped up in my brain again. The door to the room was a little bit open, so I stood there for a second, just breathing.

What was going on with Rena? What *was* Rena?

Questions, questions.

Rena

I had felt sick all morning, but not from the attack yesterday. The more I thought about it, the more I realized it hadn't been my allergies that knocked me flat under that apple tree. It was anxiety. Terror. Maybe even stupefaction.

I couldn't stand it one more minute. I had to tell Faye and Hali, even though that was another thought that made me want to barf. But when Mr. Locke left, my mouth opened and the words poured out.

"I know why Stazy is away today," I started. "She's afraid to be around me. She's afraid because . . . " And I just let 'er rip. I told Hali and Faye, my BFFs, about the meetings with Stazy and about how lonely she was. I saw Hali's face, and I saw Faye's face checking out Hali's face, but I just kept going. I told them about the magic tricks and the Adam's apple wings. Then I took in one big from-the-diaphragm breath and told them that at the apple tree, Stazy had seen me fly.

"I'm sorry," I said. "I'm so, so sorry."

Faye's almond eyes were darting between me and Hali. I tried to keep my eyes on hers, 'cuz I surely didn't want to look at Hali.

"Oh, Rena." Finally, Hali's voice *made* me look. "Rena. What if she tells? You don't even know her. All this time, we've made sure no one ever knew that you're an . . . "

That was as far as she got. The door pushed open and we all shut up, expecting Mr. Locke.

But it wasn't Mr. Locke. It was Stazy.

Hali

Stazy. Stripy-legs, creepy black clothes, eyes like basketballs behind those ridiculous glasses. And was she panting? She seemed to be panting! Before I could figure out how to wipe up this mess, she was speaking.

"I won't tell anyone. I promise."

So she'd heard everything. Not only had she seen Rena fly, but she'd heard everything we'd said just now. I had no time to think, but I tried to claw back through my memory, anyway. What exactly had we just said? How much had she heard?

Stazy continued. "I wouldn't do that. I know what it's like to be different. I know what it does to your life."

Different? What did she really know about being different?

Faye surprised me. "Uh, we're not talking about dyslexia-different here, Stazy. This is a whole different kind of different." Even for Faye, that was a good one.

"I know that," Stazy said quietly. "I know what you're talking about."

"You think so, do you?" I said. I was madly trying to read her, to see if I should go with fudging or honesty. The stakes were so high; I had to get this right. I knew Faye and Rena would follow along. For some reason, Stazy looked sad and a little scared, so I made the decision. And I went for broke.

"Rena is an angel, Stazy. This isn't about having funny clothes or a weird voice." I flicked my eyes to Rena, who looked even paler than usual, but she nodded her head at me. "We're talking about being an angel."

Stazy's voice was a whisper. "And we're talking about being a witch."

Faye exploded, all that energy roaring around the room. "She's not a witch, Stazy! Get your creatures straight." Then she made kind of a snorting sound—very unattractive, really—and said, "Witch! What are you talking about? You can't just throw everyone into a big pot of *supernaturalness!*" She looked right at me. "I know that isn't a word, Hali. Now isn't the time."

Stazy's voice was even quieter now. "I get what Rena is. An angel." She looked for a moment at each of us, then added, "*I'm* the witch."

All the air in the room was sucked into nothingness. Our three heads swivelled and landed on that stripy-black creature. The four of us just stared at each other.

And *then* Mr. Locke opened the door.

Faye
What had she just said? Witch? Did she say *witch*?

Rena
Witch. I will not wheeze. *Breeeeaaathe.*

Witch. I will not wheeze. *Breeeeaaathe.*

Dang! I knew I'd read her right. Stazy belonged with us. She *was* one of us.

Breeeeaaathe.

Hali
I know what I heard. I heard witch.

I did hear witch, didn't I? *Dratted ears!!*

Stazy
"How are those synonyms coming, guys? Stupefaction. Good word, right?" Mr. Locke glanced into our notebooks; Hali's full of print, Faye's with a couple scrawls, Rena's totally empty. I hadn't even got out my notebook yet. "Have a seat, Stazy. You checked in at the office?"

I nodded and plunked into my chair, keeping my eyes down.

Mr. Locke started talking about the math lesson in our regular class the day before, waving around the worksheets he'd just copied that were supposed to help with that. He was going on and on about decimals, how logical they were, how we'd find it easy if we just thought it all through.

It occurred to me that I'd like to just concentrate on decimals at that moment, however out-of-character that was. Just to think about dots and numbers. Imagine if decimals were my biggest problem?

Faye

Focused on math, Mr. Locke was just not reading the room. He was probably thrilled that all eyes were on his worksheets. There was so much held breath in the room that it felt like we could do a group-explode at any minute. He plodded on, smiling and encouraging us, as always. Wonderful Mr. Locke.

After a few minutes, Stazy leaned back in her chair and closed her eyes. When she opened them, they were moving around, watching the air over my head.

Of course. My bee. Stazy had seen it, she'd always seen it. Of course.

A witch, yes.

Definitely a witch.

Hali

As always, it was up to me. What were we going to do?

Logical, methodical, practical. That was me, right? But I felt like my logic had flown out the window. Ouch. Flown. *So* not funny.

Stazy, a witch? What were the chances an actual witch would find us three?

But why would she say that, otherwise? And it would explain those clothes.

And I had to admit. I *did* believe in witches.

The rest of the day was horrible. Any time I looked at Rena, Faye, or Stazy, they were either freakishly pale or tinged with green. Legs and hands were fidgeting wildly, there was a lot of eye-rubbing and staring out the window. Faye, already an expert at all those things, was outdoing herself.

My head was too muddled to even think. I just plodded along all morning, brain frozen on the words "angel" and "witch".

Rena

I didn't eat one cotton-pickin' mouthful of my carefully-prepared, allergen-free lunch. Faye and Hali didn't touch theirs.

Wherever she was, I doubt Stazy did, either. I was worried about her. I was worried about me. I was worried about all of us.

Faye

Lunch was almost over. Nobody was saying anything. Even Hali seemed to be too shell-shocked to speak.

But I guess I had more experience with shell-shock because I felt like I knew how this was going to have to go.

"I think we need to talk to Stazy. Today." Rena and Hali slowly lifted their heads, like a water ballet of depression. "And I think we'll need candy."

"Candy?" Hali said, like she'd never heard of it.

"Yup, candy." No one said anything, so that was it. Decided.

"I'll tell her. The candy store, right after school," I continued. I was in charge, I suddenly realized. I was calling the shots!

Hali and Rena's heads bobbed again, in perfect time.

I got up to find Stazy.

Stazy

I was too nervous to even look for Adam's apple wings at the candy store.

Faye bought a big bag of stuff to share, and we sat down on the curb outside the store. It was me, Rena, candy bag, Faye, Hali. Then

Hali switched with Faye, so she'd be able to hear better. She didn't look quite so much like she could spit nails at any moment, but she was very, very quiet.

We all put candies in our mouths and pretended we were chewing them.

Finally, Faye spoke.

"So, here we are. I think we know that Stazy isn't kidding, right? She's a witch. And we totally know that Rena isn't kidding."

Rena opened her mouth a little bit to say a weak, "Heavens, no!" I could see an unchewed green gummy lying in there.

"And we can't go backwards, and unlearn what we know," Faye continued.

"And we can't pretend we don't know it," Hali threw in, her bossy genes starting to wake up again.

"True," I said. What could I say? I was the Fourth Little Pig, the Fourth Billy Goat Gruff. I was nobody.

"But there's more, right, Hali? Rena?" Faye began. "We're in the same class. We all have reasons for working with Mr. Locke. And we all have something else."

All three heads were nodding up and down, the green-and-brown bob, the amazing red hair, and the spiky blonde wisps.

What on earth were they getting at?

Hali

Stupefaction. Twice in one day.

But in a flash, I knew that Faye was right. We had to do it, even though it was risky, risky, risky. It was all or nothing.

"Right." This was against everything all of us had been taught, warned, begged, and threatened about. Our parents would have meltdowns.

I decided it was my turn first. Even though I loved being first, *this* felt different.

"Yeah, so, um . . . " So not good! Boring, repetitive, noninformative. I tried again.

"I'm a . . . " I paused, because it was like the word was a big vitamin pill, stuck in my throat.

"Mermaid!" Rena squeaked. "Hali's a mermaid." The word was still stuck in my throat, so it was just as well that Rena had blurted it out. And she was on a roll!

"And Faye, too. Well, I mean, not a mermaid. Faye is *not* a mermaid. Right, Faye? Can you imagine . . . Faye a mermaid?" Rena was babbling, kind of out-of-control.

Faye blew air up through her greeny-tinted bangs and finished off our candy summit with three little words.

"I'm a fairy."

Part 5

Stories

Rena

You know that saying, *Be careful what you wish for?* Yup. That was me. I'd spent weeks wishing I had the guts to talk to Hali and Faye about Stazy, wishing she could be one of us. Little did I know—she *was* one of us.

So that day, when our threesome became a foursome, I felt a huge weight lift off me. I liked Stazy so much, and I knew Faye and even Hali would get there, too. So mostly, I wanted to leap up about every five seconds and sing one of my Glory Be! gospel songs.

But now we had four secrets to keep, not just three. At least we three had all agreed, long ago, not to tell each others' parents about our identities. I probably felt worse about that than anyone, as I knew my dads thought it would be good for me to find others like myself, to have a community. But I'm pretty sure they meant other angels, not an assortment of fairies, mermaids and now, witches. We also knew that the fewer people who knew, the safer we were. So we kept quiet.

And yes, there was one other reason we didn't tell our parents. We were scared. We were afraid that if our parents knew, they'd make us give each other up, for our own safety. They'd switch our schools, they'd move away. We were afraid that to protect us, they'd pull the lifeline that ran between us. And that couldn't happen.

Now I knew why I'd been so drawn to Stazy, right from the start. She was like us, *really* like us in the most important way; she was one of us. Like Hali and Faye, she had one human parent and one supernatural parent. Being adopted, we weren't totally sure that I was exactly the same, but it seemed likely.

Maybe I'd sensed that in Stazy, that she was supernatural, too. Faye and Hali? Why hadn't they sensed it? I'd guess for Faye it was because she was so jumpy at school most of the time that her instincts were shut right down. Of course, there'd been her bee, which should have been a red flag. Well, a black-and-yellow flag.

But Hali? Could it be that being surrounded by air had shut down her intuition? Hali was a water creature, for sure.

Hali

With the luck of the hereditary draw, I was the only kid in my family who was a merperson. My brothers had all been born human, in spite of the fact that our dad was a merman, living as a human.

I must admit that every once in a while, when I heard Evan and Clayton talking to non-existent Guy, the thought would cross my mind that maybe they had something supernatural going on, too. Could having a sea creature for a dad do some weird translation on your DNA to make you able to see someone no one else could see? But most of the time, I was sure they were just annoying little brothers, making Guy up.

I'll bet you're wondering how my family knew which of us were and were not in the Magical Mystical Mermaid Club. Easy! Mom and Dad knew the chances were high that at least some of us would be, so as each of us were old enough, we'd go to a secluded beach, and Dad would carefully take us into the water. Two years before me, Barnston had been first. All he did was flap around in the water a little, flop into the sand, slap his little fists around in the waves.

And then it was my turn. It was my first and only time in the sea. I was only three, but I still have a clear memory of stepping slowly into that blue water, holding Dad's hand. We inched forward, Mom watching from the beach, holding both Dad's and my precious hearing aids. The water was at my ankles, shins, thighs. Each time the tide pulled a wave out, I could feel a part of me crest off with it. When I felt it start to lift me, I leaned forward into it and let it hold me in its arms. Even my three-year-old self knew that this felt like another parent, like a welcome home. I dipped my head and managed to slip my hand away from Dad's; I started to head out and down, to a watery world that was beckoning me in.

It was bliss. Bliss because I moved through that water like nothing, without even thinking. I had no idea, of course, but behind me, my legs were pulsing, evolving from two limbs into one tail. And my ears! I could hear everything. Gurgles from the sand below, whispers from shells and weeds and the odd burble as tiny flashes of silver fished by me. This was my world.

Or it *was*, for the fifteen seconds before Dad caught up with me, wrapped his arms around me like a loving vise grip, and swam me back to Mom. She was hysterical, having seen the pair of us dive down and glide away from her so quickly.

It was over that fast. I was dry, in my car seat with my aids back in before I knew it. Dad drove home, Mom sniffled. My three-year-old self, strapped back into my life with seatbelts, hearing aids, and legs, wondered what the heck had just happened.

It was the last time I was ever at a beach. Each time one of my little brothers was the right age, my parents took him there, but this time, I knew Dad was holding that little hand tight, tighter than he'd known to hold onto mine. But it never happened again. No more lunges for the deep blue. Of course, I never saw this for myself. I was always safely at home, where the ocean couldn't reach me.

So no beach vacations for the Jordans, no lying on tropical sands, watching the waves tickle our toes. They'd never exactly said, but I think my parents' game plan was to anchor me so firmly to this earth life that even when I was old enough to make my own decisions, I'd choose this home.

My dad explained about our hearing aids, that our loss was because of the air we lived in, instead of the water our ears had been made for. But he was pretty quiet about his first life; every once in a while he'd tell me a tiny bit, just enough to keep me from going crazy with the not-knowing. And some stuff, I'm not even sure he knew. About our tails, for instance. Would they just reappear every time we were in the sea, every time we needed them? Or did they have a best-before date or a use-it-or-lose it clause? I wanted to know everything, but what I got were mermaid scraps.

And I know they edited it all for my brothers. The front story was that Dad was an only child whose parents had died, and that his family had been estranged from their extended families. That was my parents' way of explaining why we never visited any of Dad's family. I was the only one who knew the back story, and I was the only one who would ever be able to visit. Were they ever going to tell my brothers? I didn't know. I had enough to think about.

The sea pulled me, even though I was never near it. Heck, even the lake pulled at me, but I knew that wasn't the same thing at all. I could still remember that feeling, being lured down into a salty world where I could glide and dip.

And hear.

Faye

It was one of those rare nights when Mom was home, Ginger was home, I was home. Well, *I* was usually home, but Mom's office kept her busy many evenings, and Ginger had this lesson and that club. She had friends clamouring for her attention, day and night. My sister was a star.

On the other hand, I had two friends. No! I now had THREE friends!

It sure was nice to have both Ginger and Mom there as I tried to absorb the Three Musketeers becoming the Four . . . Beatles? Hogwarts Houses? Of course I didn't say a word, but just having Mom and Ginger there, being squashed in between them on the couch, was enough. It was like someone rubbing ointment on my jumpy heart.

Mom had been reading to us forever, and whenever she had the chance, she still did. Of course, Ginger could read super well now, and could easily have read any of the books we chose on our own. But it was *our* time. And we didn't just read. There were ideas to discuss, characters' decisions to agree or disagree with, all kinds of stuff.

The only thing missing was Dad, who had loved books, too.

He died when Ginger and I were five, and it had been us three ever since. Mom and Dad had met at medical school. I'm not sure how she broke the news to him that she was a fairy, but by the time we came along, they lived an easy and comfortable mix of fairy and human. The fountains, the faun holding the mirror, and the butterflies on our walls blended with soccer memorabilia and Dad's drum kit. Some things were about magic and some were not, and somehow it rarely got complicated.

The most complicated part was that like my friends and their families, my family was super careful to keep our secret from the rest of the world. It was like this: in a time when Rena's two dads had just been accepted, we didn't feel like risking the news that our pointy-ish ears were for a reason and we could turn into butterflies or frogs, if we felt like it.

Okay, one more teensy complication. My magic seemed to come in blasts, and sort of did things the way it wanted. Most of the time, it seemed to be in control of me, instead of the other way around. But not Ginger. Hers was steady and controlled and predictable, like her.

But here's the thing about our powers: it was usually like the time Mom asked us each to magic the house ready for our seventh birthday party. Ginger touched her fingers to her temples and soon there were tropical vines with pink and purple flowers all over the room, tiny matching butterflies flitting from flower to flower. It looked perfect. Then I closed my eyes and thought for a second and WHAM! A giant unicorn pranced into our living and took a huge drink out of the fountain, sloshing water everywhere. Each time it blinked, silvery bubbles squeezed from its eyes and floated to the ceiling, where they left tiny stars.

The thing was, I hadn't exactly thought of that; I had kind of an idea of what I wanted, and that's how it turned out. If I'd tried to conjure it again, I might have ended up with a hippopotamus sneezing rainbows. Mom said Ginger's magic was precise and controlled and mine was creative and random, but they were both excellent.

Our life was just fine, except for the hole where Dad should have been. Sometimes I couldn't imagine how Mom felt, doctoring other people every single day, making them well when neither she nor Dad had been able to take care of him. I knew she had tried everything, but in the end, cancer had been stronger than magic.

Mom's voice trickled on, leading us through the minds and hearts in the story. I realized I'd been pulling a Faye, thinking about something else when I should have been hanging in with the book. But then one more idea snagged on my brain—how weird it was that I still missed the fourth person in this part of my life, but now had a chance to have a fourth in another part.

That thought just settled onto me for a moment, then I tucked it away for later, and returned to Ginger and Mom and our book.

Part 6

Hanging Out

Stazy

Mom and I were making chili. Browning beef, chopping tomatoes. Dicing onions.

But my head was exploding. Mermaids! Fairies! Angels! I was still getting used to the whole witch situation (witch *sitch*?), and now here I was, dropped into a supernatural stew. It was hard to concentrate on cooking, but I did love chili—*mmmmm*, all that yummy meat!—so I was trying.

"Could you pass me the pot of beans, Staz?" Mom asked, wiping her hands on her "I'd Rather Be Writing" apron. I did, but my brain had switched from the Supernatural Channel to the List Channel. I ran over the list items for the millionth time, looking for clues. I knew I was acting crazy because I didn't get that much time with Mom, just to hang out. But my brain couldn't seem to stop thinking about either my "interesting" new friends or the list.

Or that flashing neon sign in my brain that said, "October 31".
That was the day the list was "due". Yuck. Sounded like homework. But when I'd asked Abuelita, she'd said that it had to be Halloween. When else? So if it wasn't done for this year, I'd have to wait until next. NO WAY!!

So, back to the list. "Key to nature", item number four. What was that? Something to do with saving the earth; like, there wasn't going to *be* any nature if we didn't take care of the planet, so saving it *was* key. Or it could be a pair of binoculars or running shoes or anything you'd need on a hike.

What about "a sweet nibble"? A cute mouse eating cheese? Donuts? A big fat wedge of apple pie with two scoops of French vanilla ice cream?

And then there was "two locks from whence you came". That seemed easy, but so weird. From whence I came—what was with the old-fashioned language, anyway?—was the house we used to live in. So was I actually supposed to go steal the locks off what was now somebody else's house? And exactly how would I do that, not exactly being a locksmith. Or was I just supposed to take a picture of them. Or a rubbing? I knew I wasn't supposed to use magic on the list. As Abuelita had said, magic was fair game anywhere else in my life, but getting into the magical world by using magic was apparently a no-no. So standing on the sidewalk of my old house and attempting to blast two locks off was out of the question. Drat.

I'd already spent a fair bit of time thinking about my magic, and about how I'd want to use it and not use it once it was dependable. I guess the option was there to use it to change how Mom and Ryan felt about magic, but I knew I wouldn't do that. That seemed like kind of an honour thing to me, not to betray the trust that my non-witch family would hopefully have in me. I needed to bring all this up with Mom and Dad and Ryan, but how could I when none of them would talk about any of it? The only person I could talk to about any of this right now was Abuelita. I was hoping that would change soon.

Mom was plopping tomatoes into the pot when my phone buzzed. Ryan! I darted into the living room.

Hey Staz! Whazzup?

Cooking chili with Mom. Mmmmmmm. Jealous?

I LOVE MOM'S CHILI! So . . . yeah.

When U home?

Dunno. School's tough, keeps me busy. Getting to the gym more?

Mostly just Thursdays.

How's that flip going?

It's ok. I'll show you when I see you, K?

Yup. Ok. Bye, little sis. Give Mom a hug for me.

Bye, big bro. I will, but come home soon and give her one yourself.

I clunked down onto the couch, narrowly missing a sleepy Carter. My heart felt like it was pooling at the bottom of my striped leggings. Was parkour all Ryan and I had in common anymore? He didn't want to talk about Dad or Mom or the new house or his new life or my messy life. Memories of our old life seemed to be forbidden, too. Running and leaping seemed to be the only thing we had left to talk about. It didn't seem like much, as much as I loved parkour.

I let my head rest against the couch and tucked my fingers in Carter's fur, giving him a scratch that had him purring within seconds. That soft rumble felt good, in my ears and in my thoughts. I closed my eyes for a second.

"Stazy? Have you given up on me in there?" I opened my eyes suddenly.

And there, on the mantel over the fireplace, was a photo of Ryan and me from years ago, arms around each other. We were standing in front of our old house. We were laughing, thinking we'd live there forever, laugh there forever.

I got up slowly and pulled it down, looking at it carefully.

"Mom?"

"Yes, honey?"

"This picture on the mantel, of me and Ryan. Can I keep it in my room for a little while?"

"Well . . . sure, if you want to." She was in the doorway now, wiping her hands on the tomato-streaked apron. "You miss him? Me too."

I nodded and held the photo close to my chest.

Me and Ryan, not runnin'. One down, seven to go.

Rena

Bowling was the perfect ice breaker, doggone it! We'd be lugging balls and throwing them down the lanes and watching them bounce into gutters; a little bit of time to talk and a lot of time to deal with bowling balls and strange shoes and to just get used to being around each other. Hali and Faye hadn't actually said out loud that it was a brilliant idea, but we all pretty well knew it. I called Stazy and she said yes, so I got Alex and Harlan to drop us all off on the way to the fancy-*schmancy* grocery store they liked, near the bowling alley.

Hali was up first. Somehow she'd wangled green bowling shoes from the squint-eyed guy behind the counter, so with her cropped green denim jacket and navy t-shirt and jeans, she somehow managed to look like a nerdy but cool bowling fashionista. I looked down at my red bowling shoes, reaching about four metres out in front of my knobby knees, and tried to paste down a pale cowlick I could see out of my left eye, but it was no use. I knew I was achieving more of a Bozo-Goes-Bowling look.

Hali swung the ball back as she rushed to the line, then flung it forward. It sailed tidily down the very centre of the alley, veering a teensy bit left to kiss the middle pin on its right cheek, knocking it and all its little round-headed buddies to the ground. *Kaboom*! Hali's first ball, and of course, a strike.

Stazy next. She did a strong lift and run to the line, but the ball bounced off her hand and pounded down the lane, sending little tremors back to our seats. It bounced itself into the gutter. Dang!

Then came Faye. She was choosing her ball from the ball return, looked over suddenly to her right and got her finger pinched between her chosen ball and its rolling-in neighbour. She had to pass her turn while she massaged her fingers. I sent her a little angel *oomph* to hurry her healing. Dang again!

But not for long, because it was MY turn! I took a couple huge breaths, sending oxygen into my lungs and limbs. I picked the smallest ball I could find and did my best version of lifting it and running to the line at the same time. Then I threw it forward with all my strength.

Dang! It did a slow motion plop into the gutter almost as soon as I released it. It rolled like a depressed snail about halfway down, then ran out of gas. A light came on over our lane, and the squint-eyed guy at the desk showed up with a *you-are-hopeless* look. But just as he reached our lane, my ball started to move. It crept forward at first, then switched into high gear, swung itself out of the gutter and zig-zagged haphazardly down the alley toward the pins. It blasted most of them over.

I looked at Stazy. Stazy looked at me. Hali looked at Stazy. Faye looked at Stazy.

That boy looked at none of us. He backed slowly away, his eyes on the ground and his forehead all hunched up and wrinkly.

I *knew* bowling was a great idea.

Hali

Wow. Rena's ball was motionless in the gutter and then blasting down the lane, just like THAT!

We all knew it was Stazy, of course. How?

Rena's magic was all about people and emotions and helping out. She had tossed a little Faye's way when she squashed her fingers, and she could help Stazy feel better about her bouncing bowling, but she couldn't actually move the ball.

Faye's? Well. Faye's magic could speak to animals and trees and flowers, but not bowling balls. She could maybe get the wooden alley to wobble the ball a little bit this way or that, on a good day. On a bad day, the floorboards might surge up and re-form into a tree with bowling ball leaves. Faye's magic was often out-of-this-world, even more than magic was to begin with.

And me? *Pfffft*. Just about naught. (I know, good word.) Almost diddly-squat. Apparently, I would be good with fish and dolphins and the sea. None of which I was ever around, so I was basically useless. Sometimes, and only sometimes, my magic extended to water in general. So maybe I could stem the tide if a toilet was flooding, but that was about the extent of my magic, until I could be in or near or within whiffing distance of the ocean.

How did I feel about that? How do you think? I hated it. I liked being good at things—at school, at running, at words. Just like my friends, I was a magical, but I had nothing to show for it. In fact, it was because of my identity that I couldn't hear well. Away from the sea, I had the disadvantages of being a mermaid and none of the advantages. Oh yes, unless you counted fixing the toilet.

I didn't.

Faye

We were walking home after bowling when I remembered something Stazy had said a while back in school. She'd been talking about magic tricks at the time, but even *I* could figure out now that it had been a different kind of magic she'd been talking about. "So you're actually studying with your . . . what do you call her again, your grandmother?"

"Abuelita. My Dad's family is Mexican."

"That sounds amazing. Not the Abuelita part, I mean the studying part," I said. "It's different with fairies. No lessons, not a single helpful tip. Your magic arrives when you're hatched and it grows up with you, but there's no changing it or molding it. It can change as you grow, but there's nothing you can do to alter it." I was kind of talking to me as well as the others, thinking for the first time about how different magic could be. It took me a minute to realize that Stazy had stopped behind us on the sidewalk. I turned around to where she stood, those big eyes even bigger behind her glasses.

"Hatched?" Hali and Rena just nodded and kept on walking. "Did you say *hatched*?"

"Sure. Fairies hatch. That's nothing." You could tell Stazy was pretty new to this supernatural thing. She looked like someone had gorilla-glued her eyes open.

"Some eggs have ten babies in them. Or fifteen. Or twenty." I thought I'd stop there. She could do the math.

Rena started to giggle. "Twenty Gingers, fighting to get higher marks than each other and one up each other on binder organization."

Even Hali got into it. "Or twenty Fayes, hiding squirrels in the bedroom and climbing into the Rottweiler cages at the shelter."

I thought I'd better fill Stazy in. "There were only two of us in my egg, Stazy. My twin sister, Ginger, and me. Just because you share the egg, it doesn't mean you're a twin, but it worked out that way with us."

Stazy's eyes were slowly coming unglued, I was glad to see. "So are the eggs bigger or smaller, depending on how crowded it is in there?"

"Nah. They're always about the size of an ostrich egg, Mom says. I guess Ginger and I just had more roaming room in there than most baby fairies."

"An ostrich egg," Stazy repeated. She was smiling at me, like she thought I was the greatest thing. Not many people looked at me like that, I gotta say. "So where exactly were you . . . hatched?"

"Home birth, right? My parents got a lot of razzing, being doctors and deciding to have us at home. But really . . . an egg? How would that go over at a hospital? And then twenty babies show up?"

Hali

It felt really weird, telling someone else our secret stuff. Of course, we made sure no one else was around; we'd been doing that forever, so it was second nature. But telling Stazy at all seemed dangerous. Inside my head I just kept repeating, "All or nothing. All or nothing."

I watched her carefully. She was really interested. Not snoopy, just interested. She asked Faye questions and you could almost see the little wheels flying around behind her eyes, sending information up to her brain.

And then she did this thing. It was part of her thinking, and asking questions, and working through all the information. While we were talking, we passed by a yard with a little stone wall along it. Stazy was asking about the fairy eggs, and at the same time, she tilted the top half of her kinda chubby body forward and gave a little hand push against the wall and whoosh! She was on top of it.

Then she was walking along it, balancing, and asking about where Faye had hatched. I was watching her, so I saw. I saw her take a quick look ahead, hear Faye's answer, and then she just . . . went.

She was jumping and bouncing and flipping. She moved from fence to tree to curb to lamppost. She found things to move around that I hardly noticed, and she did it all without even thinking about it. Or that's how it looked.

And this was Stazy, who couldn't think of two words to say at school, who flushed bright red at the mention of reading or writing. She was *perambulating* down the street like a circus star.

It was magic, but not the kind we'd been talking about before. This was the magic of talent and training and discipline.

My runners twitched below me. I just *loved* it.

Stazy

Shopping. Really? My new friends wanted to go shopping so of course I was going to go, but I hated shopping. I didn't care about things, or getting things, or getting the certain things that everyone else thought were cool. I'd rather jump or magic or eat.

But I did really like having friends, and being with them was a little too new to start being picky about activity choices, so I was going. Shopping.

Obviously, Mom was pretty happy about the friends, too. She said nothing when I told her I was going shopping, like it was something I did all the time.

The only plus to shopping was that I needed a present for Faye's birthday party in November. I was going! I could do surveillance while we were in the stores.

In, cruise all the aisles, and out. *Oohing* and *aahing* over crop tops and bracelets, fringed things and shell things and animal things. Watching Faye carefully to see what she picked up, what made her *ooh/aah* the most.

Faye

Ooh, those cat beds made like cocoons, that a cat would just curl up in and snuggle down. And tulip bulbs! I found ones called parrot tulips, with pink and green and white ruffled edges. They would look so *fantabulous* in our garden. Maybe I'd ask Mom or Ginger for them.

Or maybe I'd hold onto them and look super sad that I didn't have the money to buy them and one of my besties would remember that my birthday was coming up.

Hali

By the time Faye put the flower bulbs down, the plastic net package was all sweaty from her gripping them. I could tell by the twinkle in her eyes that she loved them, but I was absolutely NOT buying her parrot tulip bulbs for her birthday. She needed to ramp up her fashion game, and I was just the pal to do it.

I took a sneaky peek at her green-tinged bob, which looked like parrots were actually living in it. The sweater set and pearls from the first day of school had been a little extreme, but maybe a nice hairband to hold back the hair and some earrings to match? Faye had great little ears, kind of pointy and cool. So fairyish.

We made a stop in a sporting goods store. I checked out the runners and running gear, then slipped over to the real reason we were there. The bathing suits. Everyone else had one, but they looked through the rack carefully, pointing out the ones they liked and didn't like. It was all for me, but we all knew it was pointless. I wasn't getting anywhere near the ocean, and even if I did, I wouldn't actually need a bathing suit, would I? The idea of scales sprouting over me was a little creepy, but that and a tail would be my ocean outfit, not a bathing suit.

Finally, I steered them all toward the dollar store. We headed for the Halloween aisle, where we launched right into one of our favourite shopping games.

Rena

I was winning! I'd found a pair of shimmery wings, a halo, a floaty white dress and a fringed vest, all perfect angel gear.

Okey-dokey, so maybe the vest wasn't quite standard angel wear, but it was for me, so I was definitely counting it. Four points.

Hali found a shell bra, sparkly green-and-blue fabric they were selling as a mermaid tail—she was a little offended, but she needed the points—and a hairband with sea horses and shells glued all over it. Three points.

Faye came up with a pistachio-coloured leaf-layered skirt, a star-tipped wand and a hair wreath of ribbons and flowers. Tied with Hali at three points.

Then came Stazy. She searched out a pointed hat, a broom, a black-cat accessory, very familiar striped leggings and raggedy green fake fingertips. Five points. Doggone.

And that was only the beginning of the witchy stuff. "The witch is in" signs and figurines and witch-shaped candles; clearly witches were way more popular at Halloween than angels, fairies, or mermaids.

No bragging from Stazy, though. She'd won fair and square, but a small smile was her only celebration. She was leading the way out of the costume aisle when she suddenly stopped, staring straight ahead. She seemed to be looking at some weird hologram. When you looked at it from one angle, it was a girl, but if you shifted over a little, it was a witch.

Unbelievable! So much witch stuff. So unfair!

Stazy

There it was. Number six on the list: Two halves made whole.

It had to be, right? The picture wobbled back and forth between the witch and the girl, just like me. If it wasn't right, it should be, so I was buying it.

I think I might have been skipping on the way to the cashier, or maybe even dancing. My second item! As Rena might say, *"YEE HAW!"*

As I got my change, I pushed away the thought that at the rate I was going—two items found, six to go, only weeks until the deadline—I'd only be about three months late.

We went to the food court, which was kind of a good news/bad news thing. First off, Hali saw someone eating shrimp, which totally grossed her out. There were meat eaters everywhere, which suited me fine but made Faye queasy. And the air was full of allergens for Rena. So we bought a large tub of fries, got extra ketchup, and chowed down on something we all enjoyed and approved of at a table on the farthest edge of allergy heaven. Hali drowned her corner of the tub in salt and we all started in. Faye had lemonade (natural!), I had pop (fizzy and magical!), Rena had water (safe!) and Hali had water (and more salt!).

I was mid ketchup dip when it occurred to me that maybe, just maybe, I was allowed to have help on my initiation list. And who better to help than my fellow ketchup-dippers, new buddies and magicals.

I pulled out my phoned and tapped in Abuelita's number.

Oops. Maybe ketchup and phones weren't a great mix.

Hali

This was all moving a little fast for me. I mean, I was all in. The only way a mermaid, angel, fairy, and witch were going to make it work was by going for the gusto. (Was that a Mr. Locke word or a cheese commercial word?)

But now Stazy was calling a meeting. Stazy—the newbie! "Inappropriate" seemed like an inappropriate word to use for a friend, but still. It seemed a little, well, you know. Rena and Faye organized trips to the mall and hang-outs at the library, but usually there was only one person who organized meetings.

Right. Me.

But here we were, going back up that sidewalk past the bush-with-the-escaping-cat. It was a cute little house; pretty small, but still, cute.

Stazy's mom was at work, so it was just us and Carter. I hoped that this time, Carter would be friendly with all of us, not just Faye.

Stazy had snacks, gluten-free and lactose-free and meat-free and fish-free. And a salt shaker on the table, so she'd covered all the bases. I had to appreciate that.

And Stazy had purpose. She sat us down at her kitchen table in no time, passed everything around zip, zip, zip and then started on her agenda. All she needed was a gavel. I couldn't decide if I was miffed or impressed.

Stazy

I knew if I didn't just jump in, I'd chicken out and end up pretending the meeting was about new rules for the shopping game or Mr. Locke's sock choices. So I blasted on.

Abuelita had told me it was fine to have help with the list, as long as I *earned* each item, whatever that meant. It was pretty obvious that I needed help. I mean, it was October ninth, only twenty-two days until Halloween, and I had a total of two items: the picture of Ryan and me (*You and Ryan, not runnin'*) and the witch hologram (*Two halves made whole*). And I wasn't even sure that they were the right things.

I didn't tell Abuelita about my friends' supernatural side. I couldn't because it was *their* secret, not mine. It was a little weird to leave that out, but it made sense to me, too. There were people out there who called themselves witches, and there always had been. So for Abuelita, my friends knowing about me wasn't such a huge deal, although I didn't imagine she and the other people in my family went around advertising that they were witches. But probably some people thought they were the kind of witches who made herb medicines or paid attention to moons and tides. So that was okay. But how many mermaids or fairies or angels do you know? Right. So that stayed secret, from everyone.

It felt like my life was changing at a gallop; in the last year, I'd found out I was a witch, my parents had split, my brother had moved away, and I'd changed schools and houses. And now I had a set of secret-supernaturals for friends. I wanted my magic, all of it, which wouldn't happen until I passed the list test. I was kind of a witch-in-waiting at the moment, and since witchery had messed up most of the rest of my life, I wanted to at least have all of it, in return for everything I'd lost.

And if I didn't finish this test by Halloween, I'd never be a full witch. It was October thirty-first or wait an entire, endless year. It made me nervous, but it made me brave.

So I was telling them. Now. For sure.

I opened my mouth to start, breathing big for courage.

"I have something important to tell you." Yep, here goes.

"Would you like more gluten-free fake-cheesy bits?"

Part 7

The List

Hali

Stazy was freaked. She looked like Faye when homework was due and her backpack was empty.

And then, she pulled out that paper! The one she'd been staring at weeks ago in school. Don't tell me she was still trying to read it? Had she actually called us over to her house to work on vowels and consonants?

I flopped back against Stazy's couch, suddenly exhausted. Yowling, her cat shot out from behind me. Everyone gave me a look, but I didn't care. This Stazy thing was wearing me out. My logical head was telling me she had to be one of us, but my heart wanted our old threesome back. There were so many things I had no control over: my ocean-less life, my hearing, Barnston's tuba. I *needed* to be in charge here, and that had always worked for the three of us just fine.

But something was different with Stazy. She had started out shy, those huge eyes blinking as if the world was about to attack. But she seemed to be settling in now, her pigtails bouncing a little more and her stripes striding a little more forcefully each day.

Well, I had news for her. This was *my* group. Rena could fly and Faye could boss animals around and Stazy could—oh, who knew what Stazy could do? Turn teachers into tarantulas? Friends into frogs? *Ewwwww*.

Whatever it was, she could do *something*. I couldn't do a thing.

So *this* was mine.

Faye

When I first saw Stazy's list, my toes started to tap and my fingers found little bumpy things to pull off the pillow beside me. It was like homework. It was like one of Ginger's I'm-perfect-and-here's-how-I'll-stay-that-way lists.

I don't like lists. As soon as I do one hard thing, there's another one right behind it, and then another and another. No one ever makes lists of animals to cuddle or jokes to tell; it's always what needs cleaning or handing in or improving.

That got me thinking, though. What if I turned lists around, and made my own delicious lists of bulbs to plant and animals at the shelter to help and . . .

"Faye!" Someone was talking at me, but I was busy making lists in my head.

"Faye!" It was Hali. "Here's your paper. Start your list!" I was pretty surprised, but grabbed the sheet of paper and pencil she was holding out and started in on the bulbs, to begin with. Everyone else was writing too, but I had no idea about what. It was a lot like school, really.

Then Stazy passed her list around, so we could each have another look. And I saw that it wasn't like any other list I'd ever seen. There were no words like "study" or "vacuum" or "assignment". It looked like fun! My kinda list.

Of course, I had no idea what everyone else was scribbling down. So I had to ask Hali, who gave me the look, but then carefully explained that we were all writing lists of possibilities. She told me about Stazy's witch initiation and the Halloween deadline, and about which two she'd already solved.

As always, Hali was in charge, even on Stazy's list. But I didn't mind, because I knew Hali. She was bossy, for sure. But she was about the best friend you could possibly have. She watched out for Rena and me, and I knew she'd do the same for Stazy, once she had things settled in her heart. I could tell she was uncomfortable about Stazy, worried about the changes and the chance that a bigger group meant a bigger risk.

But Hali was loyal, and once she really let Stazy in, we'd totally and truly be four, not three. We just had to be patient. Rena looked over at Hali just then, and I gave her a big smile, 'cuz I knew she was watching her the same as me.

Hali always felt like she was in charge, but Rena and I knew there was more to us than you'd see at first.

Everybody else was either writing madly or chewing on the end of their pencil, looking for inspiration on the ceiling, so I thought I'd better get moving. I left the bulbs at the top of the page, and then started my second list.

Rena

I hoped pencils were gluten-free because I was chewing on mine like mad, in between scribblings. *Music from the ocean, made for a tale—*songs about fish?

A sweet nibble—Alex and Harlan in the kitchen on a frosted cupcakes day? *Fire and her friends*—hmmm, tough one.

When I saw the *Adam's apple wings* on the list, a memory of Stazy in the candy store popped up right away. I remembered her asking if there was a candy called that, and thinking it was kind of a funny request. It made sense now.

I was writing, Hali was writing, even Faye was writing! Stazy had looked stumped for a minute, but when we all put our pencils to paper, her face got less scrunched-up and she leaned in to scribble, too.

Of course, Hali's list was twice as long as anyone else's, when I peeked over. Hali loved a good puzzle and she loved being a good friend, and I could see she was working hard on both of those.

After what seemed like hours of wild scribbling, I knew I'd figured one out. I cleared my throat, like they do in the movies. Only in the movies, everyone magically (of course we throw that word around sometimes!) *gets* that it's a signal that you're going to say something humungous. Not so here. They probably thought I was heading into another spasm.

So I tried it again.

"Ahhheeeemmmmm." *Now* they were looking. *Now* they knew

something big was coming.

"I think I have an answer. Hot *diggity dawg*," I said. They were pretty much on the edges of their seats, so I thought I'd take them out of their misery.

"I'm pretty dang sure that *You and Ryan, not runnin'* is a piece of each of your clothing from before you did parkour together." I just left my idea there, brilliant, shining in the sun for all to admire. Amen, I wanted to shout!

Faye

Could there *be* any better friend than Rena, who could spend ages thrashing out a problem that had already been solved? That was something that I could so completely have done myself. So I gave her a huge hug, and before anyone else could tell her, I jumped in.

"Rena! Stazy has that one! You're solving a solved puzzle!" She looked so full of misery that I had to give her another hug. Nobody does misery or rapture like Rena; she's an angel, right?

I thought I'd inspire her with my best idea so far. With my record, I knew it would probably be about as useful as hers had been. "I'm thinking about *Two locks from whence you came* and I'm thinking about locks of hair, like maybe your baby hair, two pieces of it?"

No one said anything, which was usually code for "lame". Nothing I hadn't been expecting, though.

Hali

Two locks of baby hair? Two pieces of hair from your same head? Why would they ask for two? It didn't make sense. Still, it *was* Faye's idea.

"Sure, that could be it, Faye. Excellent. Peerless. Exemplary." In this case, sticking in a few of those words could distract everyone's attention from the actual idea. At least I hoped it could. "Let's all keep thinking about that one a bit, okay?"

Stazy

Hali thought Faye's idea was lousy, but it set some little machine whirring in my head. Two locks; maybe not key locks or combination locks, as I'd been thinking? Maybe locks of hair, like Faye said?

"I *am* going to keep thinking about that one, Faye." Faye sat up a bit and smiled her thanks. "I think you could be on to something."

As they were leaving, I thought of one more thing. "I'm so glad for your help, you guys. Even if no one thinks of anything, it helps just to know you're thinking about it. But my abuelita told me that it's important that I earn each one; no one can just give me an item. Does that make sense?

They all nodded. Of course it made sense; there was only one witch here, after all. Or potential witch.

***

That was about all the ideas I got that day, but I knew my friends were still thinking about the list, and it made me feel better to remember that four brains were busy on it instead of just one. And I kept having that niggly little feeling about the locks. Combination locks? Key locks? Door locks? Or hair locks?

The list had become like a song that plays over and over and over in your head, usually some horrible song that you wish you had never heard in the first place. I'd be feeding Carter some fishy-smelling cat food and *Music from the ocean, made for a tale* would pop into my head, or Mom would build a fire and we'd be munching some popcorn when *Fire and her friends* would suddenly ooze up, like hot butter.

I needed some distracting. I needed some magic.

The magic I could arrange. I asked Mom if I could spend a night with Abuelita. In one way, it seemed like taking time off from the list, which was not a good idea. The deadline was hanging over me like a hungry vulture. But my brain needed a rest, and maybe, just maybe, time with Abuelita would help me sort the list out.

And then another kind of magic happened when Rena called and asked if I wanted to shop for Faye's birthday present. I still wasn't sure what to give her, and I really wanted her present, my first present with Rena, Hali, and Faye, to be absolutely perfect. Even shopping felt like a diversion!

Talk about desperate.

Rena

We'd already been to the mall, so we decided to skip that and head to the little shopping area just past the school. It was fun to shop in stores that didn't all have the same name and the same stuff. It seemed like a good idea for Faye, who was sure one of a kind herself! In a *doggone* good way.

To celebrate this funky shopping trip, I decided to really fringe out. Shirt, skirt, boots, hat. Sure, I could fly when I wanted to, but the risk was almost never worth it. Sometimes it seemed like the next best thing was to have all those fringes flying, flying, flying.

No Western stores, unfortunately. Our neighbourhood needed one. People would flock in to get a Stetson hat or some fringy stuff. Really, what's not to love?

But there *was* a music store, which was bliss for me. I thumbed through sheet music and checked out their stock of musical instruments. I spent a long time looking at a really jazzy harmonica. *Hmmmm.*

"Do you think Faye would like this for her birthday, Stazy?"

Stazy just planted those big brown eyes on me. "You know her better than me, but, nope."

I gave the shiny metal stick one more rub, then put it back in its case. "Can you just imagine the great gospel sounds that could come out of that?"

"Exactly. So I know what to get *you* for your birthday, but for Faye?"

"Okay, okay. I get your point." She was right. "Dang."

It got me thinking, though, that we three—correction, four—were different in so many ways. Really, in lots of the ways that friends were sometimes similar, like interests and talents. Did I want to spend even two minutes in a garden, pulling weeds out from around vegetables? NO! I didn't even want to know which ones were the weeds and which ones were the vegetables. But to Faye, that was heaven. What was heaven to me, other than the obvious answer of *heaven*? Gospel music, Western movies, stuff to do with people and helping people. It even seemed to me that being a doctor or a nurse someday would be a good job for me; I could help people be healthier than I was sometimes able to be.

The sameness of being different was our big connection. My being asthmatic, allergic, and the total biggie, being an angel. Faye's ADHD and being a fairy. Hali's hearing loss and mermaidism. (Was that a word? Too bad I couldn't ask Mr. Locke!) And now, Stazy's dyslexia and being a witch. For us, these were connections closer than music or running or gardening.

These *were* us.

Stazy

When I finally got Rena out of the music store, we tried a cooking shop, then a bookstore. But nothing seemed quite right for Faye. There was a pet store and we both knew she'd love something from there, but it seemed a little much to drop a puppy or even a goldfish on her without asking her or her mom first.

So. We kept walking, and before I even realized where we were headed, we were standing in front of a garden store.

"Perfect!" Rena exclaimed. And it sort of was. Except it was the garden store my mom worked in.

But Rena had blasted in, fringes frizzling every which way.

Rena

As soon as we walked in, the lady behind the counter stopped poking flowers and greens into a vase and looked up. She had light-brown hair, mostly piled up on her head, with a few twirly pieces escaping.

"Stazy! What a nice surprise, hon." Wiping her hands down on her apron, she came out from behind the counter and gave Stazy a big squeeze. "I'm so happy to see you; your first time in the shop!" Then she turned to me. "Hi, I'm Gabby, Stazy's mom."

Jiminy! I was surprised.

I looked at Stazy, mouth closed. Gabby continued. "Of course, you probably knew that, right? Stazy told you, I'm sure."

I kept looking at Stazy, who finally looked at me and grinned a kind of goofy, lop-sided grin. "Well, I didn't exactly, Mom. This is Rena. Rena McIntyre."

"Hi, Gabby. It's super nice to meet you."

Then there were questions about this and that: school, where I lived, and finally, what we were shopping for. I got the feeling that Gabby was very glad to meet one of Stazy's friends, and I really liked her. She was super friendly.

"I love it that you brought your friend in to shop, Stazy. When I was a kid in this neighbourhood, my best friend and I loved poking around here. It's always been a fun place to shop!"

"I didn't know your mom grew up here, Stazy! Hot *diggity*! That's cool."

Gabby gave us a tour of the little shop. It was one of those places that seemed small, but have stuff in every corner and on every shelf and even things piled so high near the ceiling that you'd need an angel—or a witch?—to swoop up and get them.

Thinking that made me realize, for the first time, that I didn't know about Stazy's family, about who was a witch and who wasn't, or maybe they all were. Of course I knew most of this stuff about Faye and Hali, and we'd told Stazy some of it, but it made me realize that all four of us needed to sort all that out. It would be safer that way, and if there was one thing we were good at, it was staying safe. Well, except the odd absent-minded flight into an apple tree.

"Now you two just mosey around and see if you can find something for Faye. I can even offer you the family discount, if you find something!" I was totally impressed by that cowboy word, "mosey". A kindred spirit? She was beaming. I was beaming. I think Stazy was even doing her own version of beaming.

I loved the smell, even though I didn't know much about any of the plants or the gizmos displayed around to help the plants grow or be fed or watered or whatever else it was they needed. It smelled like spring, like what the colour green would be if it was a smell and not a colour. I wanted to take a huge gulp of air, but decided to take in little air sips instead, just in case there were allergens that would get me wheezing.

We ended up checking out bulbs, remembering Faye at the mall with those bulbs she liked so much. "What were those ones at the mall, Stazy? The ones she kept talking about." They all looked the same to me, like little onions with a point, skins ready to fall off all over the place.

"Toucan bulbs?" Stazy answered. "No, that wasn't it. Something to do with birds, though." She was reaching up, trying to tilt one of the higher cartons of bulbs toward her so she could read the name. She tilted it forward, a little more, a little more . . .

Stazy
Bulbs everywhere! Bouncing off my head, off Rena's head, into other cartons.

"Ouch!" Those pointy little ends hurt. I looked over at Mom. She had a pretty good eye roll going.

"Stazy. I can help if you need something. Pick them up and I'll put them back."

"Sorry, Mom." Rena and I were down on the floor, scooping up bulbs and piling them together. I was glad I didn't have to pick out the ones that had fallen into other boxes because I wouldn't know a daffodil bulb from a parrot tulip bulb.

"PARROT TULIPS! That's it, Rena! Faye was cuddling parrot tulip bulbs." But Rena wasn't paying attention. She was still on the floor, one cheek pressed down against it. Slowly, she reached a finger under the bottom of a display case.

Mom came over, her smile back in place, and showed me where the parrot tulip bulbs were before starting on my bulb spill. "Are you okay, Rena?"

Rena's head bobbed up quickly. She pulled her fist forward and slowly opened it, one finger at a time.

"Look what was hiding under that case!"

It was a necklace, a very short necklace. It was made from a velvet ribbon with a fastener, and on the front was a strange silver symbol. I took it from her hand and turned it this way and that, trying to figure it out. Mom looked over her shoulder at it, mostly busy with the bulbs.

"That's been here since the Jurassic Age, by the look of it," she said. Then she stepped in and took a closer look. "It's strange, but somehow it seems familiar to me, as if I've seen it before." Then she laughed. "But how weird is that? I recognize a dusty old necklace lost under a cabinet for a million years? Not likely! You're welcome to it, if you want it."

Just then, I turned it to face me and saw immediately what it was.

It was wings.

My first thought was that Rena should have it. She'd found it, and she was the winged one. I handed it to her, and helped her fasten it around her neck. The purple velvet looked great with Rena's white-blonde hair, and the wings.

Wings. And it was short, so it sat right there on her throat. On her Adam's apple, or where it would be if she was a boy.

Rena was looking at me. I think she'd known before I had. I mouthed, "Adam's apple wings," and she just nodded, smiling. She was already taking it off, offering it back to me.

Somehow we picked parrot tulip bulbs and paid Mom for them.

Somehow we said the right goodbye things to Mom.

Somehow Rena knew that she shouldn't mention the list to Mom.

Somehow I had the third item on my list.

Part 8

Bad News, Good News

Hali

My running feet had brought me to the lake, as usual.

Running always felt good. And the lake was a bit like low-sodium cheese: not as good as the real thing, the ocean, but better than nothing. Of course Dad and I loved salt. Deprived of the ocean, we craved salty chips and cheeses and occasionally, when Mom wasn't looking, a palm full of salt right out of the salt shaker.

I peeled off my socks and runners and dipped my feet into the water. Cold! Even an ocean-deprived mermaid couldn't stand *that* temperature. I used my socks to dry off my pink feet and shoved them, sockless, back into my runners to recuperate.

Recuperate. Great word.

Would I ever recuperate from all these changes? Stazy, busting her way into our world. She seemed nice enough, really. And I knew I had to get over the striped leggings and boots thing. What kind of a person judged others based on their clothes? It didn't say good things about me, I knew.

But somehow, my brain understood that, but my heart wasn't quite on board. She *did* look weird, and she sometimes acted weird. And I just plain liked it better when it was just the three of us. It was safer. What would happen to us if people figured out who we were? Look what had already happened with Rena, floating up into that apple tree because she let down her guard!

She needed her guard; we all did. And I felt, in a way, like I was Rena and Faye's guard. Sure, they had their parents. But I was there when their parents weren't: at school, at the mall, around other kids. I didn't hear very well, but I had sharp eyes. I definitely noticed things they didn't. And I just wasn't sure about Stazy.

What to do?

A little black thought snaked into my brain. What if Stazy didn't become a witch? What if she couldn't find all the things on the list by Halloween, and had to stay a witch-in-waiting forever? It would be hard for her to be in our group. She'd probably be pretty uncomfortable, and maybe just want to back out. Made sense. It would be best for everybody, right?

What to do? Maybe just make sure she didn't find some of the things on the list. Maybe that would be the best thing for Rena and Faye, to make sure that happened.

Yes. It made a lot of sense, even though it was the kind of thing you could never explain to them. They were way too kind to understand doing something a little sketchy for a good reason.

And there was one more teensy little thought, slithering around in the back of my mind. I didn't let it raise its head to fully hiss at me, but I kind of knew it was there.

If Stazy completed the list, I'd be the only one who couldn't actually live their supernatural life. A mermaid, stuck on land. Being around a witch, stuck without magic, might help a little. If she did decide to stay in our group.

The thought was there, but I let it slither to the back of my brain.

Waiting patiently. Hissing now and again.

Stazy

Getting to Abuelita's was now much easier. I'd done it a couple times, so both Mom and I could relax about the bus route. It was pretty simple. I did wonder about how I might travel to Abuelita's after I was a full witch. About witchery, I knew almost nothing. Bumping around on the bus on the way there, I stared out the window at passing houses and stores while I made a list of possible ways to travel there.

My bike becoming suddenly "motorized"?

Zapping Carter to carry a mini me through the streets?

A spell taking me from my bathroom to Abuelita's?

A ride across the darkened sky on a broom? Did witches really do that?

I had a lot to learn, and that was partly why I needed to be with Abuelita. It would be impossible for me to wait until Halloween to find out all this stuff. If I didn't succeed with the list, it was going to be horrible to know all the things I *would* have been able to do otherwise, but that was a chance I would have to take. I couldn't stand the suspense.

And then, I was knocking on Abuelita's door. It felt so good to be there. My room was ready: my blanket, my books, my little lamp. My witch self, the part of me that was stretching and waking up, felt so at home.

After the hugs and a dinner of nachos, cheese, and spicy ground beef (yay!), I started in with the questions. And I had a lot of them.

How long did witches live? Forever?

Were there extreme good witches and bad witches, like Dorothy and Toto faced? Or were they more like people, a mix of both?

How did they live? Like Abuelita, who lived like a human but was really a witch? Did some live in witch groups? Were they really called covens? Witcheries?

Abuelita was patient, and answered every one of my questions. I gobbled up those answers like I had the nachos. There was even time for a little magicking before bed. I knew that tomorrow she would ask about homework (ew!) but tonight we were free to do the other kind of homework, my favourite kind.

It reminded me of parkour, the way we warmed up for magic. With parkour, it was flexing and stretching, gently waking up my muscles and parkour brain so I was ready to go. With magic, it was more like meditating, so my head was clear, so no weird leftover feelings from earlier got in there and made me turn a pineapple into a rhinoceros in the middle of the living room.

We sat on the living room floor, and Abuelita flicked her fingers a couple times to light some candles. Then some music came on, gentle notes with bells tingling that massaged my brain. We just breathed in and out together, eyes closed. In and out.

It was usually hard for me to concentrate on stuff like this, but not with magic. I just kept breathing, letting that music settle my thoughts down, so easy.

After a while, Abuelita lowered the music and asked me to open my eyes and think about the word "safe". I did. Then she asked me to hold my hands out, palms up, and keep thinking about that word. I did. I could feel that she sprinkled something powdery on my hands. I sneezed. But after a few seconds, I could feel a pull on my fingers, like some energy was pulling them out. I didn't peek, though.

My fingers felt long and webby, like they were trailing out all over the room, all over the world. It was creepy and great at the same time. I tried to forget the creepy part and just keep thinking about "safe".

And then—*plonk!* In my right hand was a favourite book from down the hall. A second later, Abuelita's old housecoat hung itself over my left arm. I opened my eyes in time to see the blanket off my bed floating through the air toward me and my hot chocolate mug careening out of the kitchen in our direction. Abuelita started to laugh and flipped out her hands, sending it all back to its cupboard, shelf or closet.

"Bravo, Anastasia!" She leaned over and held my face between her hands, her eyes searching mine. "You have so much power, already. I am impressed."

"Impressed with *me*?"

"Yes, of course! Your magic is coming in so fast, now that it's started." She was slowly getting up, huffing a little. Once up, she looked down at me and said, "I wouldn't be surprised if one day, you are one very powerful witch, *querida*."

Wow. Powerful. After feeling powerless over almost everything in my life, that word was like a double burger and Carter and my new friends all rolled into one . . . heaven.

Just before I fell asleep that night, snuggled into my bed, I noticed a framed photo of a baby on my night table. Kind of strange, 'cuz I hadn't seen it there before. I wasn't even sure who it was. Not me, so maybe Abuelita? Or Dad? One of his siblings? Inside the frame in a separate section was a little curl of dark hair. Whoever the baby in the picture was, they had lots of it, so one little snip wouldn't have made any difference.

I wanted to ask Abuelita about it right then. Somehow it seemed important. But I was tired, so tired. I could feel my brain losing the thought, my eyes closing.

Tomorrow. I'd remember tomorrow.

Rena

Saturday morning. In my room, door closed. Singing, singing, singing. Heaven!

My gospel choir, Sounds Sweet, was having its annual afternoon Halloween concert soon. Gospel music and Halloween had no connection, but we always had one then anyway. I was pretty picky about my music and hoped never to be forced to sing a gospel tune about trick-or-treating or candy overdose. Soul music was bigger than that.

I'd been practising like crazy. Rehearsals were getting really intense, as they always did right before a performance. And this time, I had a solo part!

I loved everything about singing, including the pattern of learning new music. When we first got a new song, we listened to it a couple times, then tried it out with mistakes popping up all over the place. We'd sing it in our separate parts first. I was a soprano, the highest part. I always thought soprano mistakes sounded louder and shriller and more painful than any other part's.

Then we started to nail it down and mistakes became less frequent and more embarrassing. At that point, we only sang in our separate parts if we goofed. I was a dang good sight reader, which means I could read the musical notes on the page and turn them into tunes right from the start.

So we were working hard at rehearsal, plus I spent extra time with

Jazmine, working on my solo. And that wasn't even counting the time I spent in my bedroom, belting out my part, working with my breathing, making sure my top notes were top notch. *Yee haw*. This was gonna be good.

I'd decided I wanted my friends to be there. Of course, when my dads got wind of it, they got into planning mode and pretty soon it was the concert followed by a Halloween feast at our place. They were happier than pigs in muck.

And I was, too. Because my grand plan for the dinner was for us to share that information I knew we all needed. How could we have each others' backs' if we didn't even know how those backs worked?

So I sent out the text:

Faye! Hali! Stazy!

Pleez come to my place on Sat Oct 24 at 1:30 for my Sounds Sweet concert at 2:30

My dads will drive us, then making us Halloween dinner

We need to talk!!!

I liked it. A bit mysterious, a bit bossy. Now *I* was calling a meeting. First Stazy, now me. Wow. *Whodathunkit?*

Hali

Whaaaaat? Now Rena was calling a meeting? Had the whole world gone crazy?

Before I knew it, that little black thought was back. Also before I knew it, my brain was creating a text to send to Stazy.

My fingers started tapping.

Stazy

I was halfway through a highly awesome breakfast with Abuelita when my phone started buzzing. Lots of things were different between being at home and at Abuelita's, but one similarity was no phones at meal time. So I could hear those little buzzes calling me over, but I had to let them wait. I focused on my bacon and eggs.

I knew the homework train would be pulling into the station after breakfast, so I used the time between mouthfuls of bacon to ask about the list. It was exactly two weeks until Halloween, and my panic train was also starting to head into the station. My first worry was how Rena had basically found the Adam's apple wings necklace. Wasn't I supposed to "earn" every item?

"You are worrying too much about these, Anastasia. You *did* earn it," Abuelita said, swirling her toast around over her plate to pick up all the egg.

"But Rena was down on the floor! She's the one who found it."

She looked at me for a moment, then picked up one of her pieces of bacon and gave it to me. "Which wouldn't have happened if you hadn't spilled all those bulbs. You caused that chain of actions to start. It was fate." I crunched my way through her piece of bacon and hoped she was right.

Then I remembered I'd brought the necklace with me. "Do you want to see it, Abuelita? Or should I say, is it okay for you to look at it early? It won't . . . " I didn't even know what it might do, but there had to be a ton of rules about this pre-witchery stuff.

"No, it won't turn you into a scorpion or blow all the electricity out in the apartment. Let's see it!"

Wow. Scorpions. All the electricity. What great ideas she had.

I got the necklace from my room and tried it on for her, pointing out that it sat at exactly the right spot where an Adam's apple would be. I felt like I was a cheerleader for my own list. Abuelita just smiled.

When I took it off, the silver wings did a little twist under my fingers and ended up facing backwards. The wings were small so it was hard to see, but there was something engraved on there. Maybe two things. Abuelita rummaged for a magnifying glass, and I pointed it at the wings.

"It's an F. And a B. FB." I peered closer. It was so tiny! "No, there's another line at the bottom of the first letter. It's an E. EB."

"Well, I guess someone with those initials used to own it.

Interesting to think of who that person is, how they lost it, where they are now? Maybe quite the story," Abuelita said. "But it's yours now, AM."

As I handed the magnifying glass back, Abuelita said, "I want to talk to you about your list party, Anastasia. On Halloween night, when your list is complete, I'd like to celebrate. And since your new friends have been so much a part of this, I would like them to come, too."

I felt kind of sick even talking about it. I only had three things, with two weeks left to go! But even so, wouldn't my initiation be a witches-only, black cape event? I tried to ask the question as politely as I could.

Abuelita started to laugh. Again. "Oh my goodness, your initiation will be later, Anastasia. This is just a little celebration for us and for your friends." Aha! I was right; black capes to follow.

"Here's the thing. We're trick-or-treating, taking Hali's little brothers around the neighbourhood. Could we come over after?"

We sorted it all out and were just pulling out the dreaded homework backpack when I remembered those two phone buzzes.

One was from Rena, letting us know about a gospel concert and a Halloween dinner.

"I'm going to another Halloween party next week, Abuelita. And a gospel concert!" Abuelita's grin told me how pleased she was that I had these friends. I knew Mom and Dad would say yes, so I texted a quick yes and thank you to Rena. Then I went on to the next text. From Hali!

Hey. Thinking about "Music from the ocean, made for a tale". Maybe that music with waves in the background that people use to relax, you know? Meditative.

I texted back, *Hey. But what about the tale part?*

Probably not that detailed. Don't sweat it. HTH.

THX. Good idea.

But was it? It seemed funny to me, Hali leaving out part of the clue. I showed Hali's text to Abuelita, who didn't say a word. She just lifted one eyebrow, very high, and then pulled out my spelling book.

Less spelling, more spells. That's what *I* was thinking. Maybe I should have been thinking more about Hali.

Faye

What was not to love about Halloween? Even for almost-too-old kids like us, it was perfect. Dressing up, wandering around the neighbourhood at night with a million other kids *and* free candy. And now? Two parties to look forward to!

On the other hand, what was there to love about Monday mornings?

Nothing. Well, starting the day with Halloween planning on the walk to school did help. A little.

We'd just picked up Stazy at her house. Rena repeated what she'd told Hali and me about the menu for her after-concert party. Her dads were amazing. Stazy said she had no idea what Abuelita would be cooking up for *her* party, other than that it would be yummy. She had to stop right there on the sidewalk and send a text to her grandma about all our allergies and other weird food stuff.

"What about costumes?" I asked. A very important issue.

"I'm gonna be a Western doctor. Or a Western kitten. Or a Western King Kong," Rena responded. With a straight face.

"Pretty interested in having those fringes in there, Rena?" I had to say it. Rena looked at me with that angelic smile and a confident "Yup!"

Stazy was next. "I'm thinking about a food costume," she said, adjusting the straps of her backpack. "Bacon's my first choice, but I'm not sure how to make that."

Bacon. Gross. But I didn't say it.

"Maybe you could be bacon and Rena could be western eggs?" That was Hali, always thinking.

"Western eggs??? I don't think so," said Rena, her nose scrunched up. Fringed scrambled eggs didn't sound like much of a costume to

124

me, either.

"I'm too busy with the list. I don't really have time for a costume." Stazy's whole face was kind of scrunched-looking. This initiation thing wasn't easy. For the first time ever, I realized how lucky I was that fairies were just born fairies, without any tricky steps to get there. I'd probably still be studying for it, if there had been.

Stazy continued. "But I'll think of something easy."

Hali was quiet, just watching Stazy. Bacon sympathy or something else?

Stazy

What was going to happen if I didn't pass the initiation? Would my friends still be my friends, if I was only a witch wannabee?

I could feel eyes on me. Hali. I thought back to her text and Abuelita's raised eyebrow. Then it hit me that Hali was already in the position I was so nervous about, being kind of a mermaid wannabee herself. What would it be like to have your heritage sitting there, waiting to be used, but not be able to grab it?

I really didn't want to find out. I gave Hali a little smile, and she gave me an even littler one back.

"I'm still thinking about my costume," she said. That was it.

Part 9

Six More Words

Hali

I couldn't tell anyone my Halloween plan, even my besties.

When the bell rang, Ms. Burnside started our Monday morning with an announcement that since it was six weeks since school had started, it was time to write another six-word poem, this time about something significant from the autumn, so far. I was okay with that; I could whip one out in minutes, but I could see a lot of seat slumping around me.

Especially Faye. In September, Mr. Locke's word for how Faye got her poem had been *serendipitous*. Hopefully she wouldn't try *that* again. I decided there wasn't any point giving Rena a random evil eye, just on the chance that she'd remember not to write another angelic poem. So I just settled in to my own writing.

But what to write about? Track victories? Continuing tuba trauma? Or lists and friends and how to deal with both.

Stop it, Hali. Only six words.

Stazy

Could we just stop with the six-word poems, already? I had a nasty feeling they'd be sneaking up on us all year. Good thing Mr. Locke was around. Last block couldn't come soon enough.

Rena

I had a little throwback to my last six-word poem, and decided I'd better be more careful this time. No heavenly bliss, that was for sure.

I peeked at Hali. At least she wasn't giving me the evil eye as a reminder.

Faye

Oh no. Six more words. I'd been lucky last time, but didn't think I could pull another genius poem from out the window. What was Mr. Locke's word for that? Something about Sara and dipping, I think. I didn't think Sara was going to be dipping out the window for me this time.

I'd actually have to write the stupid poem.

Rena

Was it my imagination, or did Mr. Locke do a slight eye roll when he heard about the six-word poems again? But of course, he had ways to help.

Before you could say, "Don't squat with your spurs on", he'd whipped out his coloured whiteboard markers and had us brainstorming our fall experiences.

I just couldn't decide. Gaining a new friend? Would that make Faye or Hali feel weird? What about my gospel concert? It wasn't until Saturday, but the poem wasn't due until next week, the day before Halloween, so I decided it was just careful planning not to write the poem until after the concert.

I don't think I'd ever found such a great reason to put off doing homework. Hot *diggity* dog!

Hali

What was the matter with three?

It was a good six-word poem, but even with that little black thought slithering around in my brain, I knew I couldn't use it. So I brainstormed along with Mr. Locke, suggesting poems about falling leaves or giant pumpkins. Somehow he knew I wasn't giving it my all.

"Those ideas are all fine, Hali, but the best poems will be ones that are specific to you, about something that really matters to you. Those ideas are more general." He looked at me, very closely. I think I squirmed. "What happened to you this fall, specifically to you, that is important enough to you to write about?"

Uncanny. Was he a mind reader? I hoped not.

Faye

I was pretty nervous about this poem, without Sara and her dipping. So while everyone else was brainstorming, I just wrote it. Like that. I thought about what Mr. Locke said about writing something specific and personal. One thought pinged in, so I grabbed it and wrote.

Pansies border the path to love.

The animal shelter, right? The pansies along the sidewalk, the love inside.

Wow. I *loved* it. Maybe I'd finally found my form of expression. It figures it would be something six words long, but whatever. I was good at it.

Stazy was peering at the whiteboard, then writing random words in her notebook. Rena and Hali were both looking out the window. Maybe Sara was out there, dipping for *them* this time?

But I was finished. For the first time ever, I had finished all my work before anyone else. Just wow.

Then a very Gingerish thought entered my mind, the first time since the kindergarten sand table that I'd ever had such a thought: I was going to write more six-word poems. Since I was a SWPG (Six-Word Poem Genius), I was going to: DO. EXTRA. WORK.

Stazy

On Monday night, Dad had called and said he missed me too much to wait until parkour on Thursday, so how about dinner on Tuesday night? When I told Mom, I could practically see her brain setting up her Tuesday night, just her and her novel manuscript and a very sketchy dinner. Probably meatless.

Dad wanted sushi and I wanted burgers, so we had burgers.

I told him about the six-word poem, and we talked about ideas for it. Mostly I think he just liked me talking about my life, about what was important to me. Before all this happened, he knew all that without asking. But now, with him away, it was harder for him to keep up. But he did, of course.

So we talked about parkour, which was always important to me. And missing Ryan. And my new friends, which was kind of tricky. I still wasn't used to the idea that I couldn't tell anyone about them being supernaturals. It was such a part of our friendship. I knew that's how it had to be, but it was so hard not to tell Dad or Mom or Abuelita.

I told him about dropping all the bulbs on my head, just to make him laugh. He said that would be a good poem topic.

"Funny's always good, Staz. Even in a six worder, funny has to be good."

True.

While Dad bent over his burger, scarfing it down as if he'd just been rescued starving from a desert island, I noticed his hank of black hair, hanging forward. Bing! I thought back to that baby photo, the one that had shown up in my room at Abuelita's.

"Dad, does Abuelita have a baby picture of you with a piece of hair beside it?"

"Does she ever! My sibs never let me forget it, because she made one for me, the first baby, but then she was too busy or tired to make one for any of the rest of them. They never let me forget it." He took another giant bite of his burger. "Why do you ask?"

Something was zipping around in my brain, some kind of important thought, but it was moving too fast for me to catch. "No reason, except I never saw it until the last time I was there. It just showed up in my room."

"*Hmmm.*" He winked. "Magic?"

We never discussed my being a witch, but that didn't bother me as much with Dad as it did with Mom. Dad was used to the witch life, and I knew that it was just taking us time to get used to me being part of it. Mom wasn't, and I doubted she ever would be. So *big* problem.

I had lots of questions for Dad about witchery. Like how it felt to be the only kid in his family who wasn't a witch. I could imagine how his parents had handled it, kindly and carefully. Just like mine were trying to do now, but with the reverse problem. But it didn't feel like the time was right to talk about it with Dad.

One thing I noticed we talked about less was Mom. Usually Dad had a million sneaky ways to find out how she was doing and what she was doing, but this time, he hardly asked at all. That made my burger sit like a rock in my stomach after I'd finished it. I knew Dad still loved her and wanted us all back together, but what if he got tired and just gave up, before she had time to get used to the witch thing and forgive him?

So I was already feeling kind of green—I know, isn't that how witches are supposed to be?—when another text from Hali popped up on my phone.

Dad didn't ask, which was just as well. How could I explain, *For Fire and her friends, what about a match in a box and all her little match friends around her?*

WHAT?!? I thought maybe my dyslexia was tumbling the letters around so I couldn't read the words right, but multiple checks produced the same words.

What a lame suggestion. What was going on with Hali?

Rena

I spent all that week reveling in my six-word poem strategy—the strategy of not doing it. I also spent quite a lot of time figuring out if there was any way I could use the same strategy with other homework, but it was pretty tricky to think of a way to avoid fractions homework based on needing the experience of an upcoming event. Like, I was going to be eating sections of a pie tomorrow night so I'd better wait to deepen my understanding of fractions before I tackled my homework? How about watching fractions of my asthma medicine get used up in my inhaler? What fraction of each night did my dads spend testing recipes for my after-concert dinner?

Or, what portion of the time did Stazy look happy when she was texting her brother Ryan, and what portion not-happy? I didn't get it. Her face was kind of like a yo-yo: smile, frown, smile, frown. What was the guy *saying*??

Stazy

> *How's my sis?* Yaaayyyy!! Ryan!!
> *Gr8!* No point telling him about the list. *U?*
> *Studying for midterms. Hate it.* Midterms. That sounded awful.
> *Which subject?*
> *All of them, but I can handle the math. English kills.*
> I had an idea. *Ask Mom! A writer!* Would he go for it?
> *Nope. I'll manage.*
> *Coming home soon?* Did they get Halloween breaks at college?
> *Christmas.* Christmas! That was forever away.
> *Maybe you could come up here for a weekend.* I had to read it twice to make sure he'd really said that.
> *Really?* Happy dance, happy dance!!
> *Sure. Let's plan after my exams.*
> *K. Good luck, bro!*

It wasn't till after he was gone that it occurred to me. Ryan was working *very* hard *not* to come home. Who had their little sister visit them at college?

Faye

We were all in our seats: Alex, Harlan, Hali, Stazy, and me. Finally the lights dimmed, the rustling papers stopped, the wiggling butts settled in. A little chit-chat by the emcee, and then the curtains swished back. There was Rena! Oh yeah, and the rest of the Sounds Sweet choir.

It was out of this world, what happened to Rena when she was singing. Even on ordinary days, she had a little something extra—that Rena sparkle. But onstage? *SHAZAM.*

She was lifted, floating. Not really, but it seemed like it. Her head was thrown back, her mouth rounded into an 'O', her arms lifted up to heaven. And that was before she did her solo!

Hali

When Rena stepped forward to do her solo, it was like magic. Her voice was silvery, rising up against the other voices like a bell. I peeked at her dads, and they looked almost as proud as I was. Faye looked mesmerized, too. I even had a look at Stazy, who also looked spellbound.

Stazy

We'd been clapping along to the music, singing where we could. But after Rena's solo, the clapping was wild. I finally had to stop because my hands were getting sore.

I didn't know much about choirs or gospel music, but Rena's concert was pretty great. Watching anybody do something they love felt good, even better when it was your friend. And the way the music set the crowd on fire? The best.

When it was over and the audience had clapped itself out, we headed for the lobby to wait for Rena. Was it possible to feel exhausted and energized at the same time? That's how I felt.

The Two Dad Halloween Feast was coming. Food would help, as always.

Rena

As usual, my dads had outdone themselves. The pizzas looked like mummies, with sunken olive eyes peeking out between crisscrossed strips of cheese. There were witch finger cookies, a fancy spider web cake and Frankenstein cupcakes. The vegetable tray looked like a skeleton! The punch had "eyeballs" floating in it!

The funniest thing was watching Stazy bite carefully into a witch finger cookie. She was a little delicate at first, but when it tasted yummy, she crunched right through it and a couple more after that, too.

Criminy! I was on Cloud Nine. (Yes, I do say those kinds of heavenly things.) I really was. My concert had been bliss. My solo was bang on, and my dads and besties were there to hear it. And now, sharing this plumb fantastic meal? I think we were all on Cloud Nine, flyers or not.

But I knew I was going to need all that zip to get me through the "chat" I wanted to have after dinner. I tried to shovel all that away while we feasted. Alex and Harlan had lots of questions for Stazy, of course. All nice questions, just trying to get to know her.

I did get a little sweaty when the topic of magic came up, but it turned out that my dads remembered *my* interest in magic tricks because of Stazy's interest. Unfortunately, the failed baggie trick came up. Everyone had a great big laugh about the water spilling out all over the floor. "Ha ha ha," I said.

Then the table was cleared, and we four headed upstairs for some girl time. I'd even cleaned my room for the occasion. Every single horse picture had been straightened, all my cowboy hats were lined up neat on my trunk, and I'd rewound my lasso four times to get it to hang right. We sat on the floor on my fringed cushions.

Meeting called to order. Gulp.

Hali

Another meeting, and this time Rena was in charge. I could feel my spine stiffen. I didn't much feel like looking for silver linings at that point, but the thought occurred to me that my posture must be awesome with all this tension and spine stiffening.

"So, I think we need to spill the beans about some supernatural details. There are four of us now, and three of us know a lot of important information about each other, right?" Rena looked quickly at

Faye and Stazy, but seemed to stare at me longer. I doubt it was posture admiration.

She went on about it being safer if we knew more about each other's backgrounds so we could present a united front. What was this—a war?? Then I thought about my texts to Stazy. Maybe it was.

But at the same time, I could see the sense of it, and I was a bit choked with myself for not having thought of it. *I* was supposed to be the creative thinker in this group!

Then Rena said something that rocked my world even more. She wanted each of us to pick an area of information that was important to us, ask the question and answer it first ourself. Rena had control, but she wanted to share it with all of us! That had never even occurred to me; even though I tried to do what was best for all of us, I guess I always thought my voice would be the best choice. Not so Rena!

She said she'd go first.

Rena

Since I knew I wouldn't have the answers to every question, I started with one I would.

"How does your magic work?" Hali snorted right away, but *doggone* it, this was important stuff! Besides, I knew why she was snorting. I tossed her a smile as I started.

"My magic is all about people, cuz I guess that's what angels do. I can heal cuts and soothe feelings and make an angry crowd happier—most of the time. Maybe some day if I have training, it'll be more dependable."

"Why no training?" Stazy asked.

"I'm adopted, so I don't know who the angel in my family is. I don't know any other angels, so there's nobody to ask for training. It's not the kinda thing you can put on a poster on a telephone pole. Alex and Harlan are supportive, but the only magic they have is being the best dads ever."

"Don't forget making the best feasts ever!" Faye chimed in.

"And Rena, part of your magic is that you can fly. That's kind of a big one to leave out."

"Oops, I forgot." I did that nervous chuckling thing.

"Okay, I'm next," Faye continued. "My magic is all about nature, about plants and animals and the wind and the sky. Fairies never have training because it's useless. Your magic is there when you're born and it can change over your life, but it's just there; untrainable."

I couldn't help it. I started laughing again. Faye and untrainable made a perfect pair. It was one of the best things about her. In a second, she started laughing, too, and pretty soon all four of us were at it.

When we were calm enough to talk again, Faye added, "Some of us have perfect, tidy magic, like Ginger, and some of us have big splotchy messes like me. Mine's more interesting." She paused and added one more thing, "And I can shape shift into animals. Most of the time." Here she winked.

Stazy

I knew Faye's wink meant something had happened, because Hali and Rena looked like they were going to lose it again, but I also knew I wasn't going to catch up on absolutely everything in one night. Since I was next in the circle, I took my turn.

"I don't know much about mine. I know that training helps, and my *abuelita* is my teacher. My magic started as blasts of mostly the wrong thing happening, but now I'm getting better at it. What I want to happen actually happens, once in a while!"

"Can you fly?"

"Is there really black magic and white magic?"

Rena and Faye had questions; Hali, none.

"I don't know about the flying bit. Not yet, anyway. And I'm pretty sure that you decide how to want to use your magic, that it's just like regular people deciding how they want to live their lives. Some really good, some really bad, and lots a big mish-mash in between."

I stopped for a minute to see if I could think of anything else. "I'm gonna be like my *abuelita*, who is one of the really good ones."

That was it. I turned to Hali.

Hali

What could I say?

"I had one magical swim, nine years ago. I felt totally different in water. I could hear, I could move like a fish. I felt . . . omnipotent. That means I felt like I could do anything." Rena and Faye were practically splitting their faces smiling at me, trying to be supportive. Because they knew what came next.

"Since then? Nothing. Unless I'm in the sea, I have no magic. Period."

Now Rena and Faye had little sad smiles, and Rena's hand floated in my direction, using a little of her magic. I didn't want it.

Stazy asked a question. I had to hand it to her; she was brave.

"Do you have any idea what you might be able to do in the sea?"

Like I hadn't thought of that a million times. At first I wanted to bark at her, but I could see by her face that she was just interested. Rena and Faye would never ask because they'd think it would make me feel worse. But somehow, it didn't. It felt like someone was taking my magic seriously, for once.

"I'm not totally sure. Actually, I'm just guessing, because my dad won't ever talk about it. He's terrified that I'll choose that life." I decided to share one idea. Just one.

"I think I could alter ocean currents and tides."

"Geez!" Stazy said. Everybody looked . . . impressed. I was pretty impressed, too. I just hoped it was true.

Faye

It felt like Hali opened up after that, and we really got going. It was like an infomercial of supernaturalness.

Hali talking about tides reminded me about lifespans, that fairies have shorter lives than humans. It was kind of hard to describe because it's a crazy complicated combination of your hatching moment—where the planets are, how the tides are. I can't remember it all. Could be how many corn chips your mother ate before she hatched you.

I also brought that up 'cuz I knew Hali knew the answer to it. She'd once heard her dad say that merpeople lived one hundred years to the day. Imagine! One hundred years! I'd probably be fairy dust by then.

Rena wasn't sure about hers, but we all decided she must be immortal. Like, she'd never die. What else could it be with angels?

Stazy told us she'd live to be three hundred and thirty-three years old. We all just stared at her.

"Then I will become my pet for thirty-three years. Carter, right? He's not just my pet. He's my Soul Vessel. And then I'll be born again as a witch."

This was the weirdest infomercial ever.

Stazy

My head was crammed full of information. It was good to think about something other than my list, but I had to admit, even when I wasn't thinking about the list, it was lurking in the back of my brain.

But, Hali could smell things in the air super well because her nose was made for the water, where smells were harder to detect. Rena suspected that her allergies and asthma were because her breathing was meant for somewhere cleaner—like, Heaven! Faye's mom had pretended to be pregnant before she had the twins by strapping a fake belly under her clothes, so no one would know the babies were in a big egg at home.

"And I remember . . . home birth?" I asked. I was good with questions.

"Duh," Faye smiled.

Rena

Faye's family knew lots of fairies, all living secretly. She said that tons of people who lived differently, or who seemed odd, were really secret supernaturals!

Hali

Rena's dads knew there was something different about her when she was a tiny baby because they could feel little wing buds on her back. The bigger signs came later.

Faye

Hali's parents met on a sailboat. Her mom was the chef, and her dad swam by and saw her. He kept following that boat until one night, he showed himself to her. Unbelievable that Barnston and his tuba came out of a love story like that.

Stazy's parents met on the bus. Both of them had their noses in books, and when they finally looked up, they realized they were reading the same book.

Rena's parents met at a cooking class . . . surprise! They said they'd only ever adopted one child because they felt so blessed with having her. That sure made sense!

And my parents met at medical school, both studying madly to make people healthy and save lives. And now my Dad was gone; that didn't make sense at all.

But a sea story, a book story, a cook story, a school story.

That was us.

Rena

I loved my concert and our dinner and our talk. We knew so much more about each other, especially about Stazy. It felt good as friends, and more secure. And it had been my idea. I felt really, really proud.

As I closed the front door on a great night, it hit me.

My excuse was officially kaput; the concert and my big night were over. The six-word poem had hunted me down and found me.

Six words will be my death.

Ha ha ha. NOT. Can you spell immortal?

Stazy

Sunday. I was kind of tired after all that gospel clapping, feasting, and secret-sharing, so I decided to hang out at home with Mom and Carter. Mom had been writing feverishly, alternating bouts of mad keyboard tapping with moments of staring off into space, her neck cricked at the weirdest angle. Sometimes I had to take a peek at the spot in the air she seemed to be staring at, to see if great ideas or word spellings were pasted there. Nope. Nothing.

Carter and I were plunked on the couch. I was madly tapping my own keyboard, the TV converter, with one hand and scratching Carter's neck with the other. It was only October but the house felt cool, so Mom had the fire going. It was cozy, just us three.

With a sigh, Mom eased the laptop lid down and leaned back in her chair. "Break time, Staz!" She was rubbing her neck; no wonder, with all that crooked-neck air-staring! "Want some cocoa?"

So we jumped up and headed into the kitchen. While she heated the milk, I got out cups, sugar, and cocoa. We both knew we couldn't just drink cocoa without a snack, so I found some crackers and peanut butter, too.

It was encouraging to me that when I was with Mom, it was easy and natural to open the cupboard, reach in for the cracker box, pull the package out, untwist the cellophane—fifty million steps, and I hadn't even touched a cracker yet! With Abuelita, I could have magicked the crackers, peanut-butter draped, onto the plate in a few seconds. Either that, or the crackers would be attached to the outside of the cupboard by peanut butter suction cups. But I knew that would improve.

But the point was that I could function pretty easily in either world, which was what I figured I'd always need, having one foot in each one.

Back on the couch, we downed the crackers in record time. Then Mom started pulling at one of my pigtails; I guess I'd somehow got peanut butter on there. See? Things could go wrong, even *without* the magic.

"Staz, do you want to try something different with your hair?"

Whoa. What a thought. I'd been wearing my hair in pigtails ever since I'd found out I was a witch. It just seemed . . . witchy. I don't even know why, but when I'd felt powerless to be part of that world, my pigtails had helped remind me of who I was. And my striped tights.

So my first thought was to bat her hand away and say, "Forget it!"

But . . . I *was* a witch. I didn't need the hair now. And it seemed like something I could do for Mom. Plus, in case of emergency, I still had my striped legs.

So I went for it. "Sure. That'd be good, Mom."

She got a brush and started pulling it through my hair. She was rattling on about different styles, and I heard her say the word "updo".

"Really, Mom? An updo and striped leggings?"

So we settled on a French braid. She gave me instructions as she pulled chunks of hair this way and that, and then poof! It was done. It looked pretty nice, too.

"Want me to try it on your hair, Mom?" So I brushed hers, and started pulling parts into the smoothest, neatest braid I could manage. It was kind of a Frankensteina braid in the end, but she admired herself in the mirror, anyway.

She was heading back to her laptop and I was pulling her hair out of the brush, getting ready to roll it into a ball and throw it out. There was a little sigh in the air, as if a thought that had been circling around my head, like Faye's bee, had suddenly decided to land.

And there it was. The thought landed. Dad's baby picture with the lock of hair at Abuelita's, suddenly appearing in my room there. And now Mom's hair, a few long strands pulled from the brush.

It was October 25th, and I had one more item on my list. The locks weren't key locks; they were hair.

Number Four. *Two locks from whence you came.*

Faye

On Sunday, I worked on more six-word poems. Extra. Bonus. Enrichment. Supplemental. (I even looked those words up to describe my extreme *nerdishness*. I didn't *look* that one up; I *made* it up).

Finally it was Monday. I had printed the winner, the all-time best of my excellent six worders, on a perfect sheet of paper, ready to hand in. I couldn't remember the last time I actually looked forward to a deadline. I hoped we'd be writing six worders all year, to keep up my streak.

Who needed Sara and her dipping, anyway?

Stazy

If I never saw another six-word poem, I'd be happy. I dropped my grubby piece of paper onto Ms. Burnside's pile and plodded back to my desk. Our row was the last to hand them in. Hali had bounced up with hers, always confident handing in her work. Rena floated up, looking a little nervous, but Faye was the surprise. Her shoulders were back, her head was high, and she made a big deal out of flipping through about ten papers at the front of the room before she put one on the pile. She peeked out from under her green-tinged fringe to make sure people noticed her up there, picking from her poetry pages. Finally she grabbed one sheet that looked much cleaner and neater than the others and dropped it onto the pile, like "No big deal. I star out like this all the time."

The day kind of whistled by after that. Maybe partly because the six worders were done—for now!—but maybe also because I had one more item on my list so my head felt a little less like it was going to bust open. But the big thing was that Faye had invited me over to her place after school. Rena and Hali were both busy, so it would just be Faye and me.

I was stoked for a couple reasons. For one, I had never been inside Faye's house, and I knew that out of all of us, hers would be the only house that showed any part of her supernatural side. Hali's parents and my Mom were *totally* against our supernatural connections and Rena's dads weren't part of hers, so our houses were just . . . houses. But Faye's? I could hardly wait to see it.

Plus, it would be nice to just hang out with Faye. I'd done that with Rena a bunch of times, and I wanted to see how it could be with Faye. Hali, I wasn't so sure about.

Anyway, we were all going to Hali's the next day to babysit her little brothers, so that would be loud and exciting. I was looking forward to quiet with Faye.

Part 10

Discoveries

Faye

I could see how stressed Stazy was with the whole list thing, so I thought some time in my back garden with the trees and the breeze would be perfect for her.

She really wanted to look at the house first, so we did. I guess I was just used to it all, but Stazy noticed the bright butterflies on the walls in the sunroom and she loved the faun mirror. She noticed all our fountains, here, there, and everywhere. Well, of course! Fairies love streams and brooks and rivers, and those were all kind of tricky to get inside a house. I told her to try putting her fingers in a fountain, and I watched her carefully to see if I could see anything change in her, but I don't think it did. Of course, she wasn't a fairy. How did witches mellow out?

I dragged her out back, past the vegetable gardens and lawn furniture to the wild part with the tall cedars and the fall flowers. They were drooping now, but still a crazy beautiful mix of autumn colours. We each sat against a cedar and ate celery and carrot sticks. I liked mine plain, but I'd got Stazy some spicy dipping sauce so it wasn't totally horrible for her.

We talked about nothing, and it was good. All these serious talks lately had left me a little wound up. My left leg was bouncing up and down a little. We talked about shows we liked and my birthday coming up. Then we both stopped talking and chewing and rested our heads against those trees. My leg stopped bouncing.

And then I could see it. I could see Stazy's whole self feel that tree giving her a huge tree hug, like they always give me. She closed her eyes.

The last thing I saw before I closed my own eyes was my bee. It hadn't been around in a while, but there it was. I nodded at it, then closed my eyes. I could hear its little buzz over my head, then down closer to me, then over near Stazy. But my eyes didn't open.

I think we were there for a while. Maybe quite a while.

Stazy

Since when does hanging out mean falling asleep? But that's what happened at Faye's. We were awake and her leg was bouncing up and down and I had that list pecking at the back of my head, and then . . . we weren't.

When I opened my eyes, I saw Faye across from me, her eyes still closed. Everything else was the same: the smell of Christmassy cedar, the weak sun slipping down and the flowers at their end, drooping.

But then something felt different. I could feel a tiny prickling on my hand, like something walking over it. Without thinking, I gave it a shake and by the time I looked down, Faye's bee had buzzed away into the flowers.

There was still something in my hand, though, even with the bee gone. I pulled it up to my eyes, slowly. It was tiny. It was a key. It was the colour of Hali's hair, bronzy-red, and had a bee, a butterfly, and a ladybug etched on it. The end was long and pointed, not like most stubby, practical keys. This one looked special.

Faye woke up and opened her eyes just as I got it. Silently, I held it up to her. I thought about her bee, tickling my hand. Then I looked at that key. I didn't know how it worked, but I knew what it was.

Number Five. The key to nature.

Hali

For some reason, I noticed that Barnston seemed to get way less babysitting duty than me. It was Wednesday, and I had just helped out with them last weekend. I couldn't even remember the last time Barnston had babysat our brothers. What was that about? Was it because I was a girl? So unfair, if so. Whenever the parental unit tried to assign him babysitting duty, he'd say he needed to practise his tuba, and every single time, they let him off. I needed to talk to them about that. Either they needed to wise up about his sneaky musical excuses, or I was going to have to find an even more annoying, loud instrument to become *my* excuse. What was louder than a tuba? The only thing I could think of was bagpipes. *Hmmm.* I could always take my hearing aids out.

But there I was, babysitting Evan and Clayton. Oh yes, and Guy. Too bad I didn't get paid for it; I could have charged them for three kids instead of two, since apparently we all had to pretend that Guy was a guy.

At least my friends were there to help. It wasn't as painful to have to pull a brother out of a tree or make sure the cheese didn't touch the apples on a kid plate if my friends were around. I just wished Stazy had been busy or sick or had a tuba allergy.

Rena

What I wouldn't give to have a brother, like Stazy and Hali. Or a sister, like Faye. Hali had three, or maybe four, if you counted Guy; she wouldn't even notice if one was missing.

Jiminy. Wrong again. She sure would notice if Barnston and his tuba went missing. Maybe I'd better focus on Guy.

Which was kind of funny because it seemed like Stazy was focusing on Guy.

"Come on, Guy. Let's go over here. I want to dig up some pirate treasure!" Clayton loved digging. Pirate treasure or worms; anything would do. He'd made such a mess in their garden that Hali's parents had designated the very back of the yard as a digging pit.

"Hali, tell Guy that Stazy is gonna be here all afternoon. He wants to play with her, not dig with us." Evan was younger and a champion whiner.

Hali's look said it all. But what was the point of her saying, for the thousandth time, that Guy was make-believe? To Evan and Clayton, Guy was their brother. So she just smiled fiendishly and stabbed her finger in the direction of the pit. The boys waited. I guessed that dang

Guy wasn't moving.

Faye was looking at the flowers and Hali was evil-eyeing her brothers, so they didn't see Stazy suddenly turn her head to the right and smile, then move her hand forward in the direction of the digging pit. It was like she was giving someone small a gentle push. And then Evan and Clayton were heading there too, with not a word about Guy. In a minute, they had their shovels out and dirt was flying everywhere. Good times.

I gave Stazy my best "What the heck?" look. She smiled again and shrugged her shoulders.

Then Hali offered us some pop, and I forgot everything else. How often did I ever get pop, with my healthy, everything-free dads cooking for me?

Stazy

That guy Guy? I had a really weird feeling about him. To everyone else, he was the annoying invisible friend. But when I looked super hard, I could see a shadow near Hali's little brothers. No face, no voice, no arms or legs, but this shadow that seemed more solid at times, then wobbly and light at others. I felt it near me when Evan and Clayton wanted to dig, and when I moved my hand toward them, I felt it pause and then move in their direction. *Hmmmmm.*

Once the boys—two of them? Three of them?—were digging, Hali offered us some pop and we plunked down on the grass. We were all talking, kind of. Really, Hali was talking to Faye and Rena and only to me when she absolutely had to. It made me uncomfortable. And then when the pop started fizzing and sugaring around inside me, it made me antsy.

So I started checking out the yard. There was a ring of logs on one side, bordering the garden, and a teeter-totter and swing set on the other. It was a big yard with a tall wooden fence and two garden sheds. And of course, the digging pit at the back.

The pop was telling me to get up and move, and so was Hali,

indirectly. So I did, and no one even noticed. After checking out the yard, I already had a path in my mind. So I moved toward the logs first, and then everything but my path pretty well blanked out. Even a parkour beginner knew that concentration was a basic. The easiest way to hurt yourself was to lose focus, and I was no beginner! I stretched out my muscles a little, and then was off.

I stepped up onto the first log.

Rena

Holy moly guacamole! We were talking, and then Stazy got up. And then we hobbled our lips (that means shut up) because what she was doing was way more interesting than what we were talking about.

She was on the logs, slow at first and then speeding up right away. And then she did some kind of leap, and she was on the top ledge of the fence, running around the edge of the yard! My eyes were bulging. There was no way I'd do that, and I was the one who could fly!

Faye

From the fence, Stazy vaulted herself onto the top bar of the swing set, where she swung in and out of all the swings. Then somehow she was on the other side on the bar, flinging herself onto the roof of the shed. I snuck a peek at Hali, thinking Stazy was about to get a blast, but Hali's mouth was hanging too far open to do any talking.

From the shed she did a flip onto the ground, then took a run at the teeter-totter and ran its length. It moved into equal balance and then down as she ran it. Then she did another flip off the other end. When she eased herself out of the crouch she had landed in, it was like she was waking up. She looked around her and saw us, as if we'd just arrived.

Hali

I felt like the teeter-totter, whooshing up and down.

Down! This was *Stazy*, who had pushed her way into our lives.

Up! I *loved* what she was doing. Parkour.

Down! *I* had no magic, but Stazy had access to her magic the second she knew she was a witch.

Up! I could already run; maybe this would be easy for me?

Down! Once her list was done, I'd be the only one without magic. That sucked. Mr. Locke would hate that word, but it was perfect.

But up. Up. UP. I could *do* this. I was going to ask her. I was *not* going back down again. I jumped up and walked over to Stazy before I could change my mind.

"Will you teach me how to do that, Stazy?" The black thought was there, waiting in the wings for the teeter to totter back down. But it wouldn't, because I wouldn't let it. Besides, it felt so much better to throw it out.

Stazy took a second to answer, and in that second I imagined throwing that black thought out one ear; I mean, my ears weren't much use anyway, so they might as well work as an ETE (Evil Thought Exit). Done.

"Sure, Hali." Now she was smiling. "Definitely!"

Rena

Next thing we knew, Stazy had Hali doing a warm-up, which turned out to be different than a running warm-up. Different muscles, I guess. Faye and I paid attention at first, but then we lost interest. I convinced her to go over to the digging pit and watch the boys. Even without plants Faye could relate to dirt, so she was in there in a flash, and I got busy checking to see if any dirt was flying that wasn't produced by either Clayton or Evan. Kind of a Guy watch. I didn't even know how to explain that to Faye, so I didn't try.

While I stared at the *doggone* dirt, I could hear Stazy talking about cat leaps and vaulting and a bunch of other stuff. She was demonstrating for Hali, then watching her try it and adjusting her moves. I knew something big was happening there; that giant iceberg inside Hali was melting, and the more Stazy inspired and encouraged her, the more that ice became just plain sea water. Hali's favourite.

Stazy

Parkour with Hali was like the first day of school, at first. The butterflies were flapping everywhere, up in my throat so I could hardly explain, and in my body so I could hardly demonstrate. But I'd beaten those butterflies before, and I did it again.

Her eyes were kind of careful at first, but once we got going, she was revved. I'd never taught anyone anything before, but surprise—I loved it! She was a fast learner, too. Pretty soon she was running the logs easily and trying to cat leap onto her fence.

I had to focus just as hard teaching as I did when I was practising, and the time just flew. When Hali's mom called from the back porch to say she was back and that it was almost dinner, I couldn't believe it. It was like Hali just woke up, too. I saw her glance over at her brothers, still busy in the dirt with Faye and Rena nearby. I guess we hadn't been the best babysitters.

"Thanks, Stazy. Can we do that again?"

But I was pretty sure we were better friends.

Hali

I felt a little guilty about leaving Faye and Rena to babysit while I had my parkour lesson with Stazy, so after they were gone and dinner was over, I went back to the digging pit to tidy it up a bit. It was a total mess; somehow they had managed to extend the edges of the pit into the garden while nobody mean (like me!) was watching. Rena was much too kind to say anything, and knowing Faye, she'd been digging around in there herself, looking for bulbs or bugs or bliss.

So I rearranged dirt. No kidding; the ridiculous things I had to do sometimes. I pushed shovels and buckets out of the garden and back into the pit and tried to pat some flowers that had been attacked, back into place. Faye's thing, not mine. She mustn't have been paying attention to my brothers either!

While I worked, I let this new feeling about Stazy settle in. I felt like I'd been walking a tightrope between the right thing and the wrong one, and had just about fallen into a different kind of pit than the one I was cleaning up. The more I thought about it, the more I knew that finally, I was heading in the right direction with Stazy. Really, I felt pretty lucky; if it hadn't been for parkour, maybe I would still be trying to think of nasty ways to prevent Stazy from getting the things on her list.

I had to admit it; that's what I had been doing. I didn't even want to think about it, but I made myself, just to make sure I wouldn't be able to think of a reason to go back there if I got frustrated again. Because of course, there were still hard things about going all-in with Stazy. I could feel the shape of our group shifting, and I was pretty sure I'd be the only magic girl without magic, pretty soon. But now I had three friends to work that out with, instead of two. That had to be better.

I was just about finished thinking and tidying. I used a shovel to dig a deep hole at the edge of the garden to replace a little bush that was lying sideways. I was no plant expert, but sideways was definitely not right.

On my last dig down, the shovel hit against something hard and stopped. I tried it again, but the shovel clunked into the same hard object. So I dug around it, making a circle in the dirt and then inserting the shovel underneath it. After a bit of angling, the shovel came up holding something round, about the size of my hand. It was completely crusted in dirt, so I rubbed it against my jeans, which were already filthy anyway.

A shell! It was one of those ones with the points at each end and a spiral shape in between. It was still grimy, but I could see that it was beautiful: pink and peach and shimmery white. What on earth was a shell from the ocean doing buried in my backyard, a million miles away from its home?

I kept wiping it against my pants as I carried it inside. It was close enough to the digging pit that it *could* just have been one of my brothers' cast-offs, buried and forgotten. But I didn't think so. I had the weirdest feeling about it, a feeling that made me know I wouldn't show it to anyone. This shell was special, and there was a reason that it had been hiding in Jordan dirt.

I just had to figure out what that reason was.

Rena

Hot *diggity*! Friday, October 30th, the day before Halloween. It was a pretty big day at our school. In the morning, we all watched the clock and pretended we were working. Us older kids weren't allowed to get into our costumes until the afternoon. The reason? It would distract us all morning!! Unbelievable. As if our costumes, calling to us from bags in the cloakroom while our eyes watched the second hand on the clock tick by, could be any less distracting. The little kids wore their costumes all day; I think the idea was that they'd end up with their outfits on upside down and backwards without a little help. That would be interesting, though. Dang!

It was 11:30. My costume had started whispering to me about 9:15, but was now screeching and shrieking, with a few loud groans for good measure.

Very appropriate. It was an all-fired smart costume.

Stazy

Almost lunch time. Almost costume time. My costume had been nibbling a bit at my brain all morning, and I had been doing a little clock watching. But mostly I was a calendar watcher, not a clock watcher.

It was October 30th, and I had a day and a half left to find three more items! How was that even possible? I had always loved Halloween and now that I was a witch, it was a bigger deal than ever. But would it really provide me with the magical *oomph* to find three items in such a short time?

Maybe I should have brought a witch costume, 'cuz it was looking pretty unlikely that I'd ever get to be a real one.

Hali

Halloween was superb, as Mr. Locke would say. I agreed. But this year, I was feeling happier inside about my Stazy resolution than I was about my costume.

My costume was fine, but not much of a secret. How could you hide a tuba?

After lunch, we met in the girls' washroom to change. Talk about crowded! Luckily, the little kids already had their capes and sheets and tiaras on, so it was just the older kids jostling for mirror position.

I didn't need it, though. I tossed on my costume without a single mirror peek. I still couldn't believe that Barnston had said yes when I'd asked if I could borrow his band uniform and the sacred tuba for today. I think he was going to say no, but when I said I wouldn't need it tomorrow night for trick-or-treating, he changed his mind.

I waited outside the washroom, clutching the tuba to my body, while my friends angled themselves in front of the mirror for a final peek. Streams of kids wound past me, headed for the gym and the costume parade.

Faye

We finally made it out of the washroom and met up with Hali and her tuba. As we walked toward the gym, I noticed that between us, Hali and I took up most of the hall. Only small-sized kids could sneak by us on either side. We were wide.

My mouth was still sore from having blown up all those balloons last night, but when I got my peek in the mirror, I could see that it was worth it. It was even worth it that I had to ask the school secretary if I could store my costume in her back room until lunch, 'cuz it was too large and too dangerous to store in our cloakroom. Certain doom.

Rena

The costume parade had started! The *Monster Mash* blasted from the speakers. We watched each class strut and creep and shimmy around, waving and high-fiving each other.

I glanced at Faye, sitting beside me. She must have been in her element; hyperactivity was in the air, and we hadn't even started on the sugar yet!

When it was our turn to parade around the gym, Faye had to help me up because my knees were wrapped so tight in bandages and fringes that they were kind of stiff.

Faye

It was a miracle Rena could get up at all. Actually, it was a miracle any of us could get up. Me with my balloons, Hali with her tuba, Stazy with her pool toy, and Rena with her bandages.

But we did. And we were awesome.

Stazy

Faye was a bubble bath, wrapped in white balloons with a goofy shower cap on her head. At her thirty seconds in the washroom mirror, she'd painted bubbles all over her face and she was wearing rubber ducky slippers.

She was very wide and very awesome. I just hoped none of those little Draculas or devils would decide that balloon popping was fun.

You know, burst her bubble.

Rena

With an inflatable pool ring painted and papered with icing and sprinkles, Stazy was a yummy-looking donut. Probably not gluten free, though. She'd painted her face brown and had a cardboard cup and saucer on top of her head. So, coffee included! For a girl obsessed with her list, she'd come up with a great costume. Imagine what she could do next year, when she had her full magic. Imagine what she could do for all her very best friends, too! Maybe we'd end up with costumes that we could actually walk in.

Hali

Rena's Western zombie costume was *soooo* Rena, but I guess we'd wrapped the bandages a little tight because she had to walk like Frankenstein, without bending her elbows or knees. It added to the creepiness, really. There was a cowboy hat! There were tattered coveralls! There were bandages, a lot of blood, and open flesh. Rena had made very good use of her moments in front of the washroom mirror.

It made me smile to think of our costume choices. Stazy loved donuts and sweet food, definitely. But Rena looked about as *unangelic* (did I make that word up?) as possible, and Faye loved dirt way more than washing the dirt off.

And my costume? Did I love tubas?

Faye

Hali in her band costume was a mystery, a very interesting mystery. I knew how she felt about that tuba, so I wondered if she had a secret plan to lose it on the way home. But really? How could you lose a tuba? Or maybe drop it down a sewer, "by mistake"? There had to be a reason why she chose it, but *I* sure couldn't figure it out.

Just before the pumpkin draw started, I tried asking. "So Hal, why the tuba? Am I missing something?"

She smiled in a very smug-and-mysterious Hali way and said, "You'll find out tomorrow night."

So, on Halloween. I tried, but I still couldn't figure it out. Besides, the principal was at the front of the gym, pulling the names of pumpkin winners out of his witch hat. Lots of kids were winning pumpkins; the little kids squealed like piglets when their name was called. The big kids sauntered up as if it was no big deal.

It was hard work, being an older kid and having to pretend that nothing, absolutely nothing, made you very excited. Sometimes for me, it was like torture, because *a lot* of things made me excited. I had a pretty good idea that I showed it more than the really cool kids.

Anyway, I didn't have to pretend not to be excited because my name wasn't called. Stazy's was, though, and she waddled up with her coffee and donut to choose the weirdest-shaped pumpkin she could find. Very witchy, I thought. Good girl!

Stazy

I never win stuff! Wow!

That *woohoo* feeling was replaced a second later by *Listomania*. Was it possible that this pumpkin, my unexpected prize, was one of the last three items on my list? When I got back to my spot on the gym floor, I showed it to Faye, Hali, and Rena. I raised my eyebrows. It was all I had to do.

Rena

A sweet nibble? How could a pumpkin be a sweet nibble? You'd have to bake it in a pie or a scone, and that seemed a bit sneaky.

No, not *a sweet nibble*.

Hali

Fire and her friends? Orange-coloured, like a flame, but that was about it. And where were the friends? The stem? That weird indentation that made it look like an ogre? (I would have grabbed a perfect round pumpkin, for sure.)

No, not *Fire and her friends*.

Faye

Music from the ocean, made for a tale? A singing, floating, storytelling pumpkin?

No, not *Music from the ocean, made for a tale*.

Just a pumpkin.

Stazy

It was my first Halloween at this school, and it was pretty fun. After the parade and the pumpkin draw, we had a class party. There were a couple of games and some excellent junk food. Of course, vegetable and fruit platters were also present, but I avoided them. Pop and chips were more my style.

After we were completely gamed, costumed, and sugared out, Ms. Burnside turned on videos for the rest of the afternoon. Then she flopped into her chair at her desk, no doubt praying for the final bell and the weekend.

We settled in for the videos. I was ready for a little rest, myself.

Hali

One of the highlights of the day was watching my friends try to fit into their desks for the videos. I could just plop the tuba on the side, but donut rings, balloon baths, and bandaged knees weren't as simple to figure out.

It was hilarious; I loved it.

But eventually, we were ready. Snacks on desk, lights out, video on.

The first few videos were snoozers. Animated Halloween stories that little kids might love, but we were *way* too old for. I checked Rena, and sure enough, she was leaning forward as far as she could at her desk with straight knees and elbows, fascinated. I guess it was the angel in her; part of Rena would always be a little kid, in the best way.

But the rest of us? Nope. Snoozers. Even Ms. Burnside's head was drooping a bit.

It was about quarter to three. Normally we'd be in Skills Class, but the magic of Halloween had rolled over the school schedule. The lights were off. The sugar was dipping. Eyes were closed.

And then the last video flashed on.

Stazy

It started with four kids, trick-or-treating in their neighbourhood. We only saw their backs, as they moved toward this broken-down mansion. Fog rolled in, something black flapped by them. Classic Halloween haunted house stuff. Around me, eyes were opening and kids were leaning in.

The kids moved up the sidewalk, whispering. Climbed the stairs. Pushed the doorbell and waited. Waited.

And then *Something* answered the door. And through *Something*'s eyes, we finally saw the front of the kids, and their costumes. One had dirt-smeared cheeks and a flowered hat, another had hair sticking up all over the place, and sparkly swirls on her face. The third had a blue umbrella with raindrops hanging everywhere. The fourth was covered in red-and-orange feather boas. In case their costumes weren't obvious enough, they had fancy little signs around their necks: *earth, air, water, and fire.*

And then came the title of the video. *Fire and Her Friends.*

I didn't have to look around to know three pairs of eyes were on me. Faye, fairy of the earth. Rena, angel of the air. Hali, mermaid of the water.

Staring at me, Stazy, witch of fire.

Item number six. *Fire and her friends.*

Part 11

Halloween

Hali

Halloween. Finally. And I almost made it onto the street with my brothers, two little ghosts, before the parental unit saw me.

"So you're meeting the other girls at Stazy's?" Mom said. She was checking out the boys' costumes, making sure their ghost hems wouldn't trip them up. They were practising their *booo's*, ready to be released onto the unsuspecting world. Our hall was dimly lit, spooked up for the trick-or-treaters coming soon. But not dark enough, so I slid out onto the front porch to wait. I turned my back to the door. *Keep looking at the ghosts, Mom. Don't look here.*

"Yup. They'll be waiting. We'd better get going."

Her voice came closer, and went lower. "Hali? What are you wearing?" I guess blue and green sequins, even from the back, were a giveaway. Maybe the tail didn't help.

When I turned around, Dad was staring with his mouth open. I had a tail, I had shells, I had green-sparkly skin. Yup. Full-on mermaid. I also had a jacket, which I'd stuffed inside my candy bag. I'd have to get pretty cold before I'd cover up that beautiful skin.

My brothers were at the door, wild to get spooking and candy-collecting. This was tricky for my parents because, of course, they wouldn't want my brothers to know there was any problem with me dressing as a mermaid. So I took the offensive.

"It's just a costume, right? It goes great with my hair, and I sure couldn't carry that tuba around all night." I hoped they weren't looking too hard at the costume, which had taken me weeks of secret preparation. Obviously, I hadn't just thrown it on when I realized I couldn't carry that tuba around, but maybe they wouldn't have time to register that. There'd be trouble later, I knew, but I just wanted this one night as a mermaid, *splishing* and splashing around in the magic of Halloween. Well, I wanted more mermaid than that, but this would have to do, for now.

They weren't happy. They definitely weren't happy, but they let me go. I may have had green-sparkly skin, but they looked slightly greeny, without the sparkles.

I felt bad, but I also felt really great.

"Wait up, Guy!" Clayton shouted as we started down the street. "If you get more candy than us, you have to share, okay?"

"*Boooooo!*" said Evan.

Faye

Rena, Stazy, and I had been waiting a couple of minutes at the corner when a swell of noise surged from down the street. "*Booooo!*" And then a shriek. It was early because the little kids needed to do their thing earlier, supposedly. Really, I think Clayton and Evan could start at six and trick-or-treat for hours, if they knew candy was at stake. But they were supposed to be home by eight. Which suited us fine because then we could head to Stazy's grandma's place for our Halloween party and sleepover.

Wow! What a night this was going to be. The only dark cloud was that Stazy still needed two items from her list, and today was the day. But I had this feeling; I had a hunch that big things would be happening tonight. I was trying to help it all along by tossing out my magic, talking to the trees and the clouds and the stars.

Which were, by the way, Halloween-awesome. It was already twilight, and just the right amount of fog was showing up, and that smoky smell was in the air. Pumpkins were being lit, and the strange and wonderful magic of Halloween was transforming everyday streets into Spooktown.

And then out of the fog came Hali. First the long, red hair glittery with shine and shells. The sequined green-and-blue tail with a gorgeous spiked shell attached, the sparkly-green skin. She. Looked. Amazing.

But—what was she *thinking*? *A mermaid?*

159

The three of us watched her approach, completely still.

Rena

Hali was so careful, so protective of our supernatural selves. How could she dress herself up as her other half? Wasn't it like waving a flag to the world? *Here I am! I'm a mermaid! Yoo hoooo . . . I'm a mermaid!!*

But then I took a look at her face, which was—I really needed a Mr. Locke word here. Happy just didn't cut it. Suddenly, an angelic kind-of-word popped into my angelic head, and I knew that it was just right. *Radiant.* Hali looked radiant. She was being who she wanted to be, more than anything else in the world. And Hali was the best and most loyal of friends, so I absolutely knew we had to give her this. A quick look at Faye and Stazy showed me eyes that were still bugged out, so I jumped in.

"Hali! You look *so* amazing." Another look at Stazy and Faye. Eyes still bugged out. The little boys were too busy *booing* and arguing with Guy, so I took a chance and whispered, "I can totally see why you'd wear that. Who would ever guess, right? And you get to be who you are, out in the world, for a whole night. I'm so glad for you!"

Stazy and Faye were waking up now, slowly nodding along with me. Catching on.

"You look unbelievable, Hali," Stazy said. Faye tried to hug her, but there was a loud *pop!* as one of her balloons met a green sequin.

And so we headed off together, the little boys leading and *booing*. We were a mermaid, a donut and coffee, a bubble bath, a Western zombie, and two ghosts. Or was it three ghosts? I could hear Evan moaning that Guy wanted to walk beside Stazy, not him. Stazy moved over a bit on the sidewalk so there was space in between her and Evan, and it seemed to work out. Weird.

I was super glad that Alex and Harlan had managed to make me a Western zombie with looser bandages. I could actually move my arms and knees now, although sometimes I'd walk that stiff armed and legged way when younger kids came by, just to be especially scary.

Faye

Well, that explained the band uniform and the tuba at school yesterday. That wasn't Hali's *real* costume. That was just something to throw on so her parents wouldn't know what she was up to for the real thing, Halloween night. I was so excited for her that I wanted to give her another hug, but I didn't want to risk any more of my balloons.

Hali

I felt like I was floating. In my case, not on air, but in water. My costumed body felt like my real skin, my real tail. It was bliss. Even the cold air on my bare skin and having to referee my brothers, make sure they said please and thank you for the candy, didn't bother me. I just knew that this was how I was meant to be.

Up and down stairs. Knock-knock. "Trick-or-treat!" Of course everyone *oohed* and *aahed* over the little ghosts, and they got their candy first. Which was just as well because even though Rena could now move her joints so the stairs were easier, it took Faye forever to get up there, and then Stazy and Faye were so wide that they didn't fit together very well on porches.

Okay, I'll admit it. Sometimes I was a little slow, too. Yes, Hali the track star was slow. Try walking fast in a tail. Not easy. So sometimes we got a little out of sync, with the ghosts running, the zombie stalking behind, the donut and bubble bath waddling, and me baby-stepping at the back. My brothers were choked because apparently Guy was more interested in Stazy than candy, but even the invisible friend couldn't bother me tonight.

We had gone a long way, farther than I ever remembered trick-or-treating before. I guess my brothers, a whole year older than last Halloween, were that much faster, stronger, and greedier. It was glorious, though, so none of us minded. The cemetery lawn displays, the scary door-openers, my green and blueness—joy!

After blocks and blocks and blocks, I checked my phone for the time. It was tucked in my tail, right beside that shell I'd found in the garden. Looking at the shell, I had the same strange feeling I'd had when I found it. That feeling had made me include it in my costume, attaching it partway down my tail. I'd just felt like it needed to be there.

What?? Seven-fifteen already? We were so far from home! I started planning a quicker route back, one that would still take us down candy-laden streets but get us to Stazy's grandma's on time. I was following after the ghosts, thinking about the route, when my legs and heart brought me to a dead halt. *There it was.* On the left, it suddenly loomed out of the fog and the tree-lined park.

The lake. Somehow, I'd let my little ghosts lead us to the lake. Rena was ahead, closer to them, while us slowpokes brought up the rear. I could see the ghosts stop and turn their heads, staring toward the lapping sound of waves. The moon was glimmering here and there, slipping past the fog, spreading the lake out in a shimmer in front of them.

They were mesmerized. Had they ever even seen such a big chunk of water before? Of course . . . once. But did they remember that one swim? No. Because of me, our family did not go near that lake, even though it was fairly close to home.

Stazy

That strange little shadow seemed close to me the whole time, until Hali, baby-stepping at triple speed, suddenly whistled past us. The shadow was bumped away for a minute, but then I had a funny sensation that it was back.

When Hali reached Evan and Clayton, she wrapped her greeny arms around them and steered them up the next street. It was only then that I saw the lake, and remembered Hali's story about how her family avoided it. Up ahead, I could see her brothers craning their necks to look back toward the water. It must have seemed like a miracle to them, all that water in one place! An even bigger miracle than free candy.

I was trying to focus on trick-or-treating, but the list kept popping back into my head. In a short time, we'd all be at Abuelita's, and I'd have to cough up my six, not eight, items. I'd spent a whole block trying to figure out how the little shadow beside me might be either *a sweet nibble* or *music from the ocean, made for a tale*, but finally gave up on that.

The six items were carefully wrapped up inside my candy bag. Maybe I'd just have to go with six, and end up being three-quarters of a witch. How would that work? I'd only be able to do magic on Halloween or in October or when the moon was full? Maybe only in stores that sold brooms or black capes? My brain felt like mud.

And then suddenly, a thought. Since I was this close and had no other option, why not a piece of Halloween candy for *a sweet nibble*? Still waddling, I reached into my bag, pulling out lollipops and licorice, trying to figure out which would be the best list item. Then my fingers found a foil-wrapped chocolate decorated with a witch flying on her broom against the moon. Perfect. Or as perfect as it was going to get.

I was still moving, but had fallen behind the rest by the time I looked up again. That was a no-no; our parents had all told us to be careful and stick together. So I did my fastest donut-waddle to catch up.

The street Hali had turned onto was super crowded. Ahead of me, there were at least thirty kids, teens, and parents milling around in the dark. It was always easy to pick out Faye and her balloons, and there was Rena, trying to scare the little people again. Kids broke off the main group and crossed the street; more people joined the pack. It was like a giant jellyfish, getting bigger and smaller, changing shape. As I got closer, I caught flashes of Hali's shimmery tail and then saw two little ghosts near the front. *Phew!* All there.

But something was funny. That little shadow, stuck beside me this whole time? It was gone. Even my list-obsessed mind had to wonder—why would it suddenly disappear? Or had I imagined that whole shadow thing?

Faye

I'll admit it. I was getting tired. Much as I loved candy, I'd used up every bit of hyperactivity I owned. Being this wide was hard work! So I picked a couple of balloons on my outside edge and pressed them against a fence until they popped. There! At least I'd fit better on the porches now.

The little ghosts wandered ahead, within the big group we'd somehow gotten attached to. I was encouraged by how quiet they were now. At the beginning, they'd *booed* at every house and every time they passed someone on the street, but they were silent now. Maybe they'd actually run out of gas altogether and we could head them home a little early. Hali was close behind them, I could see, but I was too far back to suggest she try that.

There were so many super heroes and gremlins and cows milling around, but then suddenly it was just the six of us, miraculously all caught up and on the same porch. I don't know about Guy; maybe seven?

Anyway, the ghosts got their candy first, of course, and then headed back down the stairs, even though Hali was telling them to wait up. But when did Evan and Clayton ever listen to her?

Rena

On the porch, the rest of us got our candy, said our thank-you's and turned around. The boys were already out the gate. I noticed a couple of big people standing there, wearing those kind of half-costumes that adults throw on at the last minute. *Jiminy!* Were they trick-or-treating on their own? Hopefully they'd get toothbrushes and rotten apples as treats, the cheaters.

But no. The ghosts had stopped near those adults, and one of them was lifting off his ghost hood. *Her* ghost hood. It was a girl. It wasn't Evan or Clayton. It was a girl.

I stopped dead. Hali, Faye, and Stazy were busy manipulating tails, balloons, and donuts down the stairs.

"Hali?" I said. She looked up at me from a few stairs down, so I pointed at the ghosts, both with their hoods off now. Both girls.

Stazy

Hali jumped the stairs, even with the tail. She was on the street like *that*. Gazing desperately up and down, hunting among the costumed crowd for two little ghosts. But there were ghosts everywhere now, it seemed.

Then she was shouting, calling. We all were.

"CLAYTON!" "EVAN!" No answer. I even tried, "GUY!" No answer again. We ran up and down the street a bit, but really had no idea which way to go. How long ago had we lost them? When did we start following the wrong ghosts?

Hali started to cry, still running. People swirled around us like water, a little island of misery in the Halloween cheer.

Faye

"Hali, stop!" I shouted. She did, miraculously. We stood close, terrified. Well, we stood as close as we could when one of us was a bubble bath and another a donut. I had an idea, but we needed to be huddled before I could say it out loud. I grabbed the end of a lollipop and started popping my bubble bath while I whispered.

"We can't just run around. We need to figure out where they'd go."

"But how?" Hali was blubbering now. Rena was holding her hand, sending out her vibes.

"We need to do what Rena's doing. We need to use our magic, all together. Now. We need to locate them and find them."

My balloons were all flabby plastic now, so we pulled in close, all around Stazy's donut. We closed our eyes and we pulled in all the magic we could. Angel magic, witch magic, fairy magic, mermaid magic. It was bumpy at first, like digging a hole with your hands instead of a gardening trowel, but then it smoothed out. It felt like our brains were fused, like the little island we'd created was not just a place, but also an energy. I'd never ever felt anything like that before. The fog and the costumes swirled by us. We melted together.

And then suddenly, Stazy stepped back. "I know where they are," she said, in a whisper.

"They're at the lake."

Hali

Of course. I bent over, grabbed the end of my tail, and gave it a violent twist, ripping the tail right up to my thighs. No more baby-stepping.

I shot off. Of course, they were at the lake. Why hadn't I thought of it? Still crying, I dodged crowds and leapt curbs. I knew my friends were behind, but I didn't look back to check how far. I knew they'd be there.

My brothers had no memory of ever seeing the lake before; it was magical to them. It had pulled them back just like it did me. But I could swim, without ever having been taught. They had no idea. Faster. *Faster.*

As I ran, I tried to summon any magic I had to keep those waters back, away from my little brothers. My head was working as hard as my feet, but I was pretty sure it was useless. My only magic was my speed.

Faster.

Stazy

Parkour helped. I wasn't as fast as Hali, but I was right behind. I'd pulled the plug on the donut and was jumping and landing as I ran.

I was magicking, too. I could feel Evan and Clayton at the lake. They were definitely there; I could feel their amazement. I could feel a little fear, too.

I was afraid to attempt it, but I was trying to hold them back. At least, I think I was. Hopefully I wasn't pushing them in? I called on Abuelita to help; I called on anyone in that witch world I was so desperate to enter to help.

The list wasn't important. None of that was important.

RUN.

Hali

I could feel Stazy behind me now, closer. I could feel waves of something strong coming from her direction. I knew what she was doing.

RUN.

Faye

I was a ways behind Stazy. There were less people, now. My balloons were flapping pathetically. I was sending out everything I could, to the fog, to the trees at the lake, to the stars. Hold them back. Please. Hold them back.

A ghost came out of a gate and shouted "*BOOO!*" at me. I wanted to *screeeeaaaam* back, but I was too busy moving.

RUN.

Rena

Of course I was at the back, getting wheezy, but running as hard as I could.

I was talking to someone, making deals. God? I don't know. Whoever. I was bargaining a lot of stuff away if only Evan and Clayton were safe.

The delicious spook of Halloween seemed like a horror movie now, blurry as I ran past. The clowns looked murderous and the puppies had fangs. Even the angels looked devilish.

I kept pushing, far behind the others. I saw a pack of ghosts. It seemed like they were all laughing at me.

RUN.

Stazy

Suddenly, my feet felt wet. Very wet. But the ground was dry.

"HURRY"!" I screamed.

There was no one around, now. We were almost there.

Hali

I could see it, now. I could see the lake. And I could see fog. But nowhere, nowhere could I see my brothers.

"CLAYTON! EVAAAN!"

My breathing was ragged, but I couldn't bend over to rest. Stazy pounded down the sand to where I was.

"They're in the water. My feet were wet first," she gasped, "but now it's up to my shins."

Faye

I waited for Rena, then helped her down to the beach. She was wheezing big time.

We stood close together again, shouting and staring into the fog, afraid to choose a direction in case it was the wrong one.

Stazy

Screaming wasn't helping. Staring into the thick fog wasn't helping. We were just gonna have to split up and run both ways.

And then, I felt a sharp tug on my right arm. I looked there, and of course there was nothing. When I didn't move immediately, the tug came again, harder. This time, I did move.

"This way, you guys. They're this way." Nobody asked how I knew; I guess nobody cared. We started to run along the water's edge.

My feet were wet again, this time with real lake water.

Hali

My hearing was terrible, but there was nothing wrong with my eyes. Through the fog, I finally saw a wisp of white a little way from shore.

I splashed near it and lunged.

A sheet. Just a sheet, floating.

My breath came in and out so fast now. The fog was in my brain.

"KEEP GOING!" Stazy yelled. So I did.

Stazy

The tugging was getting lighter now. Were we almost there?

Or were we too late?

Hali

And then the fog cleared a tiny patch, and I saw a head. And then two heads.

They were in the water; I couldn't see how far. The water was icy, but I threw my hearing aids on the beach and dove toward them. Maybe there was a tail involved, maybe there wasn't. I didn't care. I could feel the pull of the lake, the pull of the water, but I ignored it. The pull of my brothers was stronger.

When I dove under, I could see them clearly; I could even hear them. They were laughing.

Stazy

She was in the water and had them before I could even see them.

And then they were back on the shore, all three. Shivering and crying. Rena and Faye had caught up. We were all shivering and crying. There was no time to be mad or even to go back for the candy they'd left farther back on the beach. We had a search party for Hali's hearings aids, almost lost in the sand. Then Hali, Evan, and Clayton each peeled off their top layer of clothing, and Faye, Rena, and I gave them our dry outer layers.

We headed off the beach, teeth chattering, but otherwise, silent.

The little shadow was back, close to the boys.

Rena

The scene at Hali's house? Not so pretty. Her parents were fairly hysterical. Who wouldn't be?

Of course, they weren't just dealing with three water-soaked, frozen kids. They were also dealing with the story they didn't think we knew, about Hali and the lake.

But after they'd calmed down a bit and realized that Hali hadn't done anything worse than lose sight of which ghosts she was following, their focus switched to Evan and Clayton. Who *had* just wandered away from us and headed back to the lake on their own. Now they were chattering, candy-less little boys with tear-streaked faces.

I lifted my hands a bit and squirted some angel joy. Everybody here really needed it. And we did *not* want Hali to be grounded so she couldn't come to Stazy's grandma's.

And then the weirdest thing. I heard a little voice, one I'd never heard before, whisper "More, please!" Evan and Clayton were busy peeling off wet shoes and sweaters; it wasn't them.

But it was a kid voice. I looked at Faye and Stazy. We were crunched up against the door in the front hall, trying to let the Jordans do their thing, but hanging in there for Hali. I shot out a little more love.

Then, as the little boys headed down the hall for dry pajamas and hot chocolate, I saw Stazy's arm lift and her fingers uncurl and release something. It was like she had been holding someone's hand and had just let go.

And the same little voice said, "Thank you." Wow.

Hali

I didn't like to lie, but I had to be pretty sketchy about how we'd found my brothers. *We just had a feeling they were at the lake* sounded pretty bogus, but it was the best I could do, even though my frozen brain had been rolling the story around all the way home.

And really, it wasn't that far off. The four of us had melded together and all that magic had given Stazy the feeling, the answer. And she'd had some help at the end, I knew. Guy. I was going to have to rethink the invisible friend.

I knew Rena was magicking because for once, my parents didn't see my being a mermaid as the biggest thing in the room. At least, I think that's why their focus wasn't on that. Or was it actually possible that they realized that maybe this wouldn't have happened if my brothers had been allowed to be near water or go swimming like other kids?

Whatever the reason, I hoped my family was in for a change.

And I hoped I hadn't messed up my hearing aids, lying on that wet sand.

And I hoped I was still going to Stazy's list party.

Faye

I felt like I'd been holding my breath since we walked up Hali's stairs, but finally, we were hauling our sleeping bags and backpacks into Mr. Jordan's car. Hali was *not* grounded. I think she was in for more parental *yik-yak*, but not tonight. We were off to Stazy's party!

In the car, I looked at my friends, Hali in the front seat with her dad and the three of us in the back. We were four exhausted, magic-drained post trick-or-treaters. The bandages and fringes were loose and hanging off Rena. Stazy's coffee hat had disappeared completely during our run and her donut was deflated. Hali didn't even have a costume on anymore; she'd been so cold she'd changed into her fuzzy pajamas and robe to warm up. And I looked like a carnival game with all the balloons popped, my rubber ducky slippers streaked with mud and sand.

Even hyper me was too tired to talk on the way over. Hali's dad put the radio on, and everybody basically slumped into their seat. My eyes might even have closed for a couple minutes. Being a bubble bath is hard work.

Part 12

Four Friends, Six Words

Stazy

And then we were on the street in front of Abuelita's apartment with our pile of sleeping bags and backpacks. Hali's dad watched until I'd pushed the buzzer and we'd got our stuff inside the front door. Then with a wave he was off, probably to help thaw out his sons.

I thought about that little shadow again. From now on, I was listening to my intuition. The shadow had suddenly disappeared, after all that trick-or-treating time beside me. Where did I think it had gone? Why hadn't I thought about it?

No matter, now. Now was list time, and I only had seven items. Maybe six, if my witch-wrapped chocolate was gonged. But I'd done my best. And really, saving Hali's brothers was better than any list. And I had really helped with that.

We were outside Abuelita's door, waiting for her to answer my knock when Hali started fishing in her backpack.

"Stazy?" she said. Then she pulled out a shell, pointy on both ends, gleaming pink and cream and peach in between. It was the one she'd had on her mermaid tail earlier. It was so beautiful.

"This is for you." She held it out toward me. "It's *Music from the ocean, made for a tale.* I'm sure of it."

The last item on my list! And it made sense, what she was saying. But I was afraid to take it. It looked so . . . important.

"Take it! I found it in the garden, and I'm pretty sure it's my dad's, from his life in the ocean. I think it's meant to be on a mermaid's tail."

"So . . . made for a tale and a tail, you mean?"

Hali smiled. "Yup, I think so." She pushed the shell closer to me.

"But I'm supposed to earn everything on my list. It's so great that you're giving me this, but I didn't earn it."

All three of my friends turned to me and stared.

"Are you kidding, Stazy?" Hali was the one to speak. "You might have saved my brothers' lives tonight. You earned it." She looked down at the shell. I could see she was giving up something really important to her. "Just take it, okay?"

So I did. And then the door opened, and Abuelita was like the sun, beaming down on all four of us.

Rena

Stazy introduced each of us to her grandma, but we weren't sure what we should call her. "Call me Abuelita!" she laughed. It was perfect. I already had a couple of grandmas, but I'd never had an *abuelita* before, and I suddenly felt like I needed one.

After each introduction, Abuelita looked at the girl, long and careful, like she was somehow figuring us out. Was it my imagination, or did she look at Hali longer than Faye and me? But then that huge smile spread over her face again and she ushered us and all our junk into her little apartment.

Hali

"Anastasia!" Stazy's grandma used her full name, and she stretched it out and made a beautiful *zzz* sound at the end that was like music. Maybe I'd start calling her that, too. What a name!

The living room was ready for Halloween, but in a different way. No fake cobwebs or gravestones here. The only Halloweeny decoration was a "The Witch is In" sign that Abuelita laughed about. "I couldn't resist!" was all she'd say.

The lights were all off, but the room was lit everywhere with candles and jack-o-lanterns. On the mantle, on the hearth, on every flat surface, the glow of fire flickered and shadowed the walls. The ceiling danced, a swirl of dark and light shapes.

It was perfect. What was magical and mysterious about Halloween was in that room; it was spooky, but not scary. It was just part of a magical life.

Faye

First we ate, 'cuz we were starving. There was a ton of Mexican food, and we jumped right in. I felt like I'd been on a roller coaster, and now that my feet were back on the ground, my stomach was revved up.

Then we settled in on the floor in a circle; it was almost list time, I could tell. Stazy pulled out her backpack. Abuelita watched her, the firelight flickering off her face. The way she was looking at her, I could tell that even if every single item was wrong, she would be just as proud of Stazy.

But I was nervous. I wanted them to be the right things. Stazy deserved to pass this test; she'd worked so hard, not just on this list but at our school and with us. There was a little fairy cheerleader inside me shaking green pompoms like mad.

Rena

I lifted my hand, just a little. Just a wee bit of magic to help Stazy. She'd helped Hali so much; now it was our turn to help her.

Hali

I didn't have any magic to give her now, but I'd given her the shell. And there was one more thing, something that we could all give Stazy to help with the list. I looked at Rena and Faye, and both nodded. It was time.

When I started to tell Abuelita about who we really were, I could see Stazy start to shake her head.

"Hali, no! You don't have to!" But we did. How could Stazy honestly explain my shell or the key she'd been given by Faye's bee without the story that went with it? The true story was what made them list items. Just a shell? Just a key? No big deal. But a mermaid's tail shell and a key from a magic bee?

And besides, having met Abuelita, it didn't seem nearly the risk it had when I'd told—no, asked—Faye and Rena about it. We had all agreed. It was worth the risk.

So I told Abuelita who I was, and Faye and Rena took their turns. She was maybe a little surprised, but not flabbergasted or dumbfounded. She was a witch, after all.

And then it was really time for the list. Stazy pulled out my shell first, and I hoped that meant she was super confident about it. She gave me a brave smile as she brought it out, but she did look a little wobbly.

I knew what Faye and Rena were up to with their magic; I wished I had more to give, but I'd given everything I could.

Stazy

This was it. I pulled them all out, one by one. For some, I gave a little background, to let Abuelita know why I thought they were right. I couldn't believe what my friends had just given me, a green light to explain each list item fully. But I took it.

I started with Hali's shell. I told Abuelita about finding the shell in the dirt, how Hali had known it was something special from the moment she'd first touched it. *Music from the ocean, made for a tale.* (Or tail! I was a terrible speller. So be it.)

Then I showed her the key from Faye's. Faye's bee had a starring role in that story, and so did Faye. *Key to nature.*

When I showed her the wing necklace and told her the story about Rena and me and the bulbs, she laughed out loud. We all did, but hers was the only laugh that didn't sound nervous. *Adam's apple wings.*

My parents' locks of hair. *Two locks from whence you came.*

I showed her the video, *Fire and Her Friends*, on my phone.

The photo of Ryan and me, my very first find. *You and Ryan, not runnin'.*

I had a hard time getting the hologram picture out of my backpack. It was pretty well squashed in there. The witch and the girl, back and forth, back and forth. *Two halves made whole.*

The last item, the piece of chocolate, I saved for last. Not because it was the best, but because I was the most nervous about it. *A sweet nibble.*

Well. Abuelita picked it up, unwrapped it, and popped it in her mouth.

Rena

Really? You ate list items? It took you weeks to find them, and then someone (even wonderful grandmas) just ate them? *Jiminy!* What a system!

She finished eating the chocolate, slowly. Our four pairs of eyes were darting back and forth, trying to figure out if this was a thumbs up or thumbs down moment.

The suspense was killing me.

Faye

And then, just like that, Abuelita said, "Anastasia, welcome. Your list is complete." She gave a little wink and said, "And number three was delicious!"

I was the first up. Hey! I'm hyper! It has to be good for something.

We jumped up and down and screeched. We made way more noise than you should in an apartment, and Abuelita didn't even care.

Stazy had made it. She was a witch!

Hali

There was a moment, just a moment, when I felt what I'd been afraid I'd feel for so long. Jealous. Alone. Left out. But my friends saw it, and all together, we pushed that feeling away. Maybe we used a broom or an angel wing. Maybe it was a giant cedar branch. Or maybe we used a mermaid tail. But after a moment, it was gone.

Stazy was a witch! We'd done it.

Stazy

Abuelita wanted a picture of us. While she was framing us on her cell phone, she said she wanted a photo of *fire and her friends*. We were Fire, Earth, Air, and Water.

Rena

It was the most amazing photo. All four of us with our arms around each other, candles, and jack-o-lanterns casting eerie light. Bits of face paint left on us, a mess of droopy balloons, deflated donuts, fringes and pajamas. Four huge smiles.

Hali

Four of us.

Faye

And then Stazy made the weirdest suggestion.

"Trick-or-treating is done. Lake rescue, check. Food, list: check, check. How about a party game?"

Personally, I was whacked. Sleep sounded good to me. But one game before we jumped in our sleeping bags? Okay!

"How about we each write a six-word poem about tonight?"

WHHHAAAT!?! Since when was writing a six-worder a party game? I mean, I was an expert, but there was a limit.

But it was Stazy's celebration, so we did.

Stazy

I'd made it. I was a witch. At long last. And I didn't know exactly what that would mean, how it would affect the rest of my life. But I knew it was a huge part of me. I'd accepted it, and now my family needed to do the same. But that was for tomorrow.

For tonight, I needed to say something to my friends, to Abuelita, and I just couldn't seem to get it out of my mouth. So the six-worder seemed like the next best thing.

Rena, Faye, and Hali looked at me like I was moldy lunch in a locker, but they pulled out their phones and started to compose. All was quiet for a few minutes. Abuelita started to douse the candles flames. Halloween was almost over.

Then, one by one, heads raised as their poems were finished.

Faye seemed anxious to go first.

Faye
Party homework? Rock star poets cope. Easy.

Rena
Mayhem! Ghosts, candy, lakes, shadows . . . friends.

Hali
Oh brother! Barnston. Evan. Clayton. Guy.

Stazy
List complete. Friends here. Finally home.

Acknowledgements

My thanks to Ard, for wrestling commas out of and more sense into my manuscript.

To Norma, for reviewing and giving valuable commentary on my words.

To Karen, for making my four girls and their six worders come to life on the cover.

And to Lori and Cheryl Ann, whose belief in those girls and their story magicked this book into existence.

About the Author

Nancy Hundal has written many books for young people, including the BC Book Prize-winner *I Heard My Mother Call My Name*.
She is a retired teacher-librarian who lives in Vancouver, BC, Canada.
Nancy is also a singer like Rena, a lover of nature like Faye, a cat-person like Stazy, and hearing-impaired like Hali.

www.nancyhundal.com